P.S. from Above

Book One: Restoration

A Novella by Jamie Karris

ISBN: 9780979416675

Cover design by Exquisite Create

Table of Contents

1 1

2 4

3 10

4 17

5 23

6 29

7 31

8 35

9 41

10 45

11 50

12 66

13 70

14 75

15 79

16 83

17 86

18 89

19 94

20 102

21 109

22 112

23 123

24 127

25 130

26 138

27 144

28 158

29 172

30 175

1

It was Friday morning in the little seaside town of Havocy Bay. Julian Noel, a handsome dark creature, was writing frantically on his note pad. He was in the little small café' he had been visiting every day since coming to town. He sat at his usual table - by the same window that gave him the best view of the town square and all of the people. Nothing disturbed him – Not even the sound of plates crashing to the floor and the cook yelling at the waitress who just wasted, in his estimation, a gourmet meal. Julian wrote and scratched out his words in frustration not noticing that a crumpled piece of paper had fallen to the floor. He threw his pencil down, picked up his coffee cup, coupled with both hands and took a few sips.

Linda Andrews, the waitress that had been serving him every day, even though you could not tell if Julian realized that or not, approached the table with his bill in her hand. She bent down and picked up the paper that had fallen to the floor and put it in her pocket. She assumed it was trash.

"Having any luck?" She asked as she put his bill on the table.

Julian looked at her name tag and responded, "Excuse me?"

"I was asking if you were having any luck." Julian just sat and stared at her. "With your writing I mean. I've noticed you are pretty intense with it. So I was just wondering."

"Wondering what?" Julian asked with an exasperated tone and returned his attention to the papers before him.

Linda responded with a smile but was truly confused as to why her question seemed to be unintelligible. "If you were having any luck with your writing."

Julian brushed her off with his silence not answering her question. He reached into his pocket and pulled out some money that was in perfect order by denominations. The cook yelling to her from the kitchen pulled Linda's attention away from Julian.

"Hey, come and pick up this order before the next millennium please!"

Linda bellowed back, "Alright, alright I'm coming. Don't get your britches all in a wad." As she turned back to the table, she saw that Julian had left, leaving the money for his bill with a generous tip. She quickly looked around for him and caught a glimpse of him exiting the café' with purposeful motion in every step.

The square was filled with trees vibrant with the colors of fall. Water fountains splashing sent up a cool mist into the air.

The young preppies, sipping on their lattes, were seated on colorful cushioned cement blocks that served as tables and chairs. In the wind, the rustling reverberation of papers turning, children laughing and frolicking – dogs barking, echoed through the air. No one noticed how the dark handsome stranger just seemed to have appeared in the square coming from no particular direction at all. Julian walked along, by himself, taking everything in. He walked over to the fountain sat on the rim and put down the satchel that was hanging over his shoulder. He took out a leather-bound notebook from it and started to make notes. He wrote down some information under a name that had already been written in the book, Linda Andrews.

2

Cameron Day ran into the building with the news journal in his hand. He hurried to the elevator knocking over a secretary whose arms were filled with documents. She glared at Cameron who tried to apologize unsuccessfully to a woman who had spent most of the night arranging those files for her tyrant of a boss. Cameron picked up one or two of the folders and handed them to her and continued racing to the elevator. He pressed the button and became very agitated when the doors didn't open fast enough.

He was pounding on the buttons when he heard a voice. "That won't make it come any faster." He looked around and saw that it was the woman whom he had clobbered running in. She was still trying to recover from the mess he had made. He turned to go back and help her when the doors to the elevator suddenly opened. He gave a look of pity to the woman and jumped in. The doors closed while the woman continued her pain-staking chore.

Simon Giles was reading from the same journal that Cameron had in his hands. He shook his head as he lowered the journal onto his desk. The elevator doors opened and Cameron ran down the hallway past Simon's office. He was almost to his destination. He reached her office just as she slapped down the journal onto her desk.

"Not again!" Salomé Davenport yelled as she was sitting there distraught and rocking back and forth in her chair. Writing awards, a diploma from Harvard and a plaque that read, Salomé Davenport – JR. Editor graced the office of the tall black beauty. Her looks lent more to that of a runway model instead of those of a 4.00 English and Composition major with a degree from Harvard. She got up from her chair and began to pace back and forth, calm but yet in a panic. She sensed someone behind her and turned to see Cameron standing in the door. "How's it going?" He asked.

She pointed to the paper in his hand. "How do you think it's going?"

Cameron walked into her office and closed the door. "What do these losers know? These critics are just a bunch of wannabe publishers who could not make it in the real game."

"I may not know what they know, but I know that I could lose my job."

Cameron moved over to her desk and sat on the edge. He folded his arms across his chest and said, "Girl, please. Mr. Giles came after you hard." He picked up one of her many awards from her desk and began to play with it. "He's put a lot of money behind you and would be crazy to let you go."

Salomé snatched the award from his hand. "Exactly! He has put a lot of money into my projects and me. And in this bottom-line world, you had better produce. And if you are black, produce 100 times as much. This is the third time that I have been trashed. The third time!"

Cameron gave her a campy smile. "Well you know what they say; the third time is the charm."

 Salomé responded in disgust. "Oh, you have jokes now. I don't feel like joking. It's my tail on the line!"

Cameron rose from her desk walked over to her and took her into his arms. "It's your talent that got you here, so your tail is just fine, oh so fine."

Salomé tried not to smile as she fell gently into his arms. He was not that big of a man at 5'9 and a little shorter than Salomé but somehow she always felt safe in the arms of her Nubian king, even if he was a little on the high yellow side.

"So you think my tail is fine." She said to him as she looked into his eyes for reassurance. With a smile on his face, Cameron said playfully, "Well let me just take a look here." He bends down.

Salomé pulled him back up. "Will you quit playing and just kiss me?"

"Gladly" he responded and they kissed. As they are kissing Cameron placed Salomé's cheek in his hand and noticed the wetness of her face from the silent tears that she began to shed.

"Listen, baby," he said in a comforting tone. "Mr. Giles knows what he is doing. He knew what he was doing when he hired you. You have to learn to trust your ability."

She pulled away from him. "I know all that but…"

"But nothing. This will pass. You will weather this storm just like all highly gifted people, heck like all people have to do and show the world who you are." He jumped on top of her desk. Salomé looked at her door to see if by chance someone was going to walk in to see her crazy boyfriend standing on top of her desk.

"Boy, get off of my desk. Have you lost your mind?"

Cameron began to yell. "You are Salomé Davenport. Top JR. Editor of Giles Publishing. You are unstoppable! Say it!"

Salomé pulled on his pants leg in an effort to get him off her desk. "Cameron, will you get down and please be quiet."

He yelled again. "Unstoppable!"

Salomé sensed that she was fighting a losing battle repeated, "Unstoppable."

Cameron continued. "Wonderful!"

Salomé repeated. "Wonderful!"

Cameron picked up the new journal and shook it in the air and said, "To Hades with what these critics say!"

Salomé was now caught up in the frenzy. "Yeah – what do they know anyway?" Their cheerleading was interrupted by a beep over the intercom. Mr. Giles deep hypnotic voice streamed out of the box that was on her desk. It made Salomé feel as if she had been called to the office by her fifth-grade principal.

"Ms. Davenport?"

"Yes, Mr. Giles?"

"Come to my office please."

Salomé began to turn pale and she tried to prevent Mr. Giles from detecting her fear by projecting a very strong answer. "Yes sir, right away Mr. Giles." She looked at Cameron who had climbed off the desk and gave her a nod.

"It's going to be o.k. – Go on."

Salomé left the office. Cameron stood gazing at her as she walked down the hall. A look of concern came across his face as he looked back at the journal and picked it up. "Dang." He whispered under his breath and he began to tear the journal apart and threw it into the garbage. He left her office closing the door behind him.

3

Salomé walked up the hallway of an empty office. Office hours began at 9. It was only 7:10 am. She always got there before the rest of the staff besides Mr. Giles. Rumor had it that he never went home. She approached his door with hands shaking and knocked on the beautiful thick Mahogany wood. "Mr. Giles?" She said not knowing if she was heard or not. There was a lump in her throat that she was sure was muffling the intonations of her speech.

"Ms. Davenport, please come in." She heard coming from the other side of the closed door. She took a deep breath and entered his office. Mr. Giles was seated but rose as all good southern gentlemen do when a lady enters the room. He beckoned her to have a seat.

Simon Giles was an intimidating figure of a man. Tall, about 6'4, elderly, but still had a body build that reflected the reasons for all of his athletic trophies that were displayed in his office. The lines of gray that flowed through his full head of thick black curly hair, representing wisdom and strength, accentuated a square tanned sculpted face. He possessed a quiet gentleness that made Salomé view him more as an expecting but supportive father than a boss. But he never played down to her. He always treated her as a formidable woman. She appreciated that very much.

Salomé looked around the office that she had been in a hundred times before. His achievements made hers pale in comparison. She sat in silence as she watched Mr. Giles read over the article in the journal. She was hoping and praying that he could not detect that at any moment she might hurl and prayed that she would not do so on his imported Persian rug.

He folded the paper and laid it on top of his desk. "So who is next on your editing meter?"

"Next on my meter?" She asked.

"Yes. Who are we going to put out next?" Salomé sat there looking perplexed. Simon laughed slightly but he tried not to make Salomé uncomfortable. "You know, who are we going to publish next? Who do you have on the table?

"You want my opinion?"

Simon looked at her sternly. "No, I don't want your opinion. I pay you for authors and not opinions. You are my JR. Editor are you not?"

Salomé dropped her head. "I don't know am I?"

"What would make you think that you are not?" He asked still looking directly at her while leaning forward on his desk with his hands folded and resting on top of the journal. Salomé did not answer. She looked at the journal beneath his hands. Simon knew that she was looking at the journal said, "Oh please don't tell me that you are letting this get to you."

Salomé spoke up. "How can I not? They have destroyed every author that I have published that we have published."

Simon threw the paper on to the floor. "Oh, Hodge pudgy. So what. If I had listened to all of my critics, I would not be here today. Ms. Davenport – you must learn to follow your God-given talent and instincts and when you do make no apologies for it."

Salomé began to roll her eyes slightly and said, "Yes I know. It doesn't matter what others think."

Simon was now a bit angry. "Ms. Davenport, I tolerate a great many things. An employee being flippant however is not one of them."

Salome said remorsefully, "I apologize Mr. Giles. But how can I follow my instincts when everyone says they are wrong?"

"Who is everyone? Are these critics everyone? Look here." He got up from his desk and walked over to a filing cabinet and pulled out a hand full of reports. He walked back over to his desk and gave her the papers. "What do you see here?" He asked.

"They look like sales figures." She answered.

"That's right and good sales figures. Your sales figures."

Salomé was in total surprise. "Mine! Are you kidding me?"

"You creative types. You need to look at these more often. It looks like to me that a whole lot of people respect your instincts."

"Just not my peers." Salomé put the reports back on the desk. A look of despondency came over her face. Simon felt for her but coddling was not what she needed at the moment. She needed to know that he still had faith in her abilities and he was determined to show her that he did.

"Ms. Davenport, I did not call you in here to discuss your peers. I called you in here because I am sending you on a field assignment."

"A field assignment? What kind?"

"There is a great writer's symposium that is held once every five years at this small seaside resort called Havocy Bay. This group gathers together some of the most gifted writers in their generation."

Simon always had a purpose in every decision that he made. He knew that this brutal business that was unkind to females holding her position - let alone a black female was burning out

Salomé. She was talented but much too young to play the political games that exist in the entertainment world - It was not that he felt that she was too weak to handle it. He was just watching out for his most valuable teammate. He needed her to get away for a while so she could find herself again. He knew she was an ace and he was not going to let her be swallowed up by waves of self-doubt.

Salomé again responded in shock. "And you want me to go?"

Simon responded with a look of exasperation on his face. "Once again, it is what I pay you for. I want you to go there and find that Pulitzer winner that I know you are going to bring to this company. Marsha has made all of the reservations for you. You leave in an hour."

Salomé jumped up in a panic. "In an hour? But I'm not packed. I'm not ready for a trip like this." Simon sat and looked at her, waiting for her to calm down. Salome' looked over at him and realized that she had lost it. She sat back down. Simon pulled open his desk drawer and pulled out a black credit card and handed it to her.

"I believe that you can get all that you need with this." Salomé took the card and a big smile came over her face.

"Well, I guess I could use this to find a few things. How long will I be gone?

"Until you find that Pulitzer winner."

Salomé let out a giggle. "Yeah, ok. Until I find a Pulitzer winner." Salomé continued to laugh lightly until she looked and saw that Simon was looking at her but was not laughing at all. Salomé panic again. "You are serious."

Mr. Giles continued to look at her. He let out a deep sigh, "Once again, this is what I pay you for. Your plane is leaving in 58 minutes."

Salomé jumped up and walked briskly towards the door. As she was getting ready to exist, she turned slowly and looked at Mr. Giles. He had returned to his writing. She smiled at him grateful that he still believed in her.

"57 minutes Ms. Davenport." He said not looking up from his work. Salomé quickly left the office.

10-year-old Dorian Andrews was walking home from school. He was humming classical tunes to himself as he was walking through his neighborhood. A bulking backpack over his shoulder and the fact that he was carrying his books in his hands lent evidence to the fact that the pack carried something else. As he was walking he heard something overhead. He looked up to see an airplane flying over him.

He stood and watched it for a few seconds and then continued on his journey. This time as he was humming he incorporated the sound of the Jet engine plane into his self-made music. He was so engrossed that he did not notice that there was a man slowly driving down the same street following him in a dark expensive car.

4

Salomé walked up to the counter of the car rental place to retrieve the rental car that Marsha arranged for her. There was a male Asian Indian customer service representative, Ravi, on the phone talking to another customer. He was most enthusiastic about his work but was much too talkative for Salomé's taste - especially since she was in a hurry to pick up her car and get to the stores as soon as possible. After standing there for a few seconds without being acknowledged, Salomé cleared her throat to get his attention.

"Just one minute Ms," Ravi responded in a heavy Indian accent. Salomé put her purse on the counter and waited for Ravi to finish. He was writing information slowly and methodically on a pad.

"You need a car for two days only? Say listen, man, if you get a four-day plan it will be just a little more expensive but you can get a convertible." He paused for a moment, not noticing that Salomé was becoming more and more agitated.

He continued. "Yes, yes that is correct." Ravi began to type something on the computer.

Salomé attempted to let out a loud sigh in the hope of gaining his attention. It did not affect the man. Finally incensed she yelled, "Excuse me!"

Ravi put his hand up to quiet her and then put his hand over the phone and said, "Yes, yes, just one more minute." He returned to his conversation. "So we have a Mustang, blue, white top, black on black, yellow with black top. We have FIAT'S, black cherry with black top. We have cars that seat 4. Say listen, man, how about a Mercedes- Benz? He paused. "We have…"

Salomé just stared in shock as Ravi continued to read off the menu of cars to the invisible customer as she just stood there.

"What kind of place has Mr. Giles brought me to?" She pondered. No longer able to take being ignored, she slammed her hand down on the counter, grabbed the phone from Ravi and yelled, "Sir, for the love of all that is merciful, I have been standing here for the longest trying to pick up a car that I already have reserved. I know that you are on the phone with a customer who obviously has time to spare. I, on the other hand, am a customer as well but I don't have time to spare. I have pressing business and I need my car now! Please!"

Ravi just stood there stared at her for a moment. Salomé asked, "Do I need to repeat myself again? I need my car!"

Ravi calmly took the phone back from Salome. "Cousin Jaffe, I will have to get back to you later." He spoke a phrase in his native tongue that Salomé was sure wasn't too flattering. He laughed and then hung up the phone. With a smile on his face, he looked at Salomé and asked how he could help her.

"My car, I need my car." She said almost in tears of utter frustration.

Ravi began typing into his computer again. "How many days and what kind would you like?"

"I already have an SUV on hold."

"You do? Well, why didn't you say so earlier? Name please."

Salomé rolled her eyes and told him. "Salomé Davenport."

Ravi began to type. After a while, the printer spat out the information. "Here you go Ms. Davenport" handing her the printout. She just put it in her purse without looking at it. "Your car will be brought around in about 20 minutes."

"20 minutes?" Salomé questioned.

"Yes, ma'am," Ravi responded with a big smile on his face.

"Why will it…" Salomé paused. "Never mind. May I just get the keys please?"

"Oh yes, ma'am as soon as they bring the car around." Salomé was going to say something else when the phone rang.

Ravi put his hand up to stop her and said to her, "One moment please" and answered the phone. "Hello," he paused. "Hey man, you need a car this weekend. Oh yes, we have some great deals for you." Ravi winked at Salomé and continued with his conversation. Salomé surrendered and took a seat.

Salomé was looking out of the window when a lovely convertible car was being pulled up to the door. She looked beyond it in the hope of seeing an SUV but did not. Now her blood was boiling. It had been well over twenty minutes. She turned to get up to go talk to Ravi but she found him standing there with keys in his hands and that outrageous smile on his face.

"Ms. Davenport, here are your keys."

"I told you that I had an SUV," Salomé said confused.

"Yes ma'am but this place is much too pretty to look at it through the windows of an SUV. Here and it is on the house. Thank you for being so patient."

Salomé took the keys sheepishly and embarrassed. She knew that she had been anything but patient. "Thank you so much and I am sorry that I blew up at you."

"No apology necessary," said Ravi. "I get wrapped up sometimes and talk too much with my customers. They become like family to me. I hope that I did not cause you any inconvenience."

"Not one bit." She said smiling. "Actually you just made my day with your kindness."

Ravi laughed and reached out to hug her. "Just to give a little bit of kindness makes our lives worthwhile." He handed her the keys and opened the door for her. "Have a wonderful stay here at Havocy Bay."

Salomé got into the car and ran her hands over the leather steering wheel. "I know that I will now." With a smile, she put the keys in the ignition, started the car and drove off with Ravi waving good-bye. As she was driving down the winding roads, she observed the sandy white beaches and the slow descent of the sun over the horizon. She began to fully grasp the truth that Ravi had spoken. This place was much too beautiful to experience from an SUV. She took a deep breath and felt her life pressures fading away. For the first time in a long time, she was beginning to feel that all was well with her soul. In her heart, she thanked her boss and a sweet little Indian man name Ravi.

5

Dorian was sitting outside on the stoop in the front of his house reading some classical music books when Linda his mother came home from working at the café. Her arms were full of grocery bags. Dorian put his books down and jumped up to help his mother.

"Dorian baby, what are you doing sitting out here on the steps?"

Dorian reached for 2 of the bags. "It was too pretty out to go inside. Besides I knew that you would be coming home soon. I wanted to be here and ready just in case you needed help with anything and I was right."

Linda bent to kiss him on the cheek. "My little man."

"Come on mom, I'm a man, not a little man. I'm 10 now remember?" Dorian said.

"Yeah, I remember." Linda bent and kissed him over and over again. Dorian pretended to protest the unacceptable behavior from his mom but doesn't do so with much effort.

"Mom will you stop it, stop it." Dorian ran into the house laughing as Linda ran in after him. Dorian put his bags in the kitchen and then remembered that he left his music books out on the stoop. He left the kitchen to go retrieve them. He ran outside and picked up his books. He was heading back inside when he was distracted by the sound of a car engine. He looked up for a second and saw an unfamiliar car driving away but he paid it no more attention. He went back into the house with his books. "Hey, mom, what's for dinner?" He yelled.

As Dorian went back into the house, the car turned the corner, drove down another street and made a right turn that put it back on Linda's street. It was the same dark car that was driving in the neighborhood earlier. It stopped a few houses down from Linda's. The man inside took mental notes of the Andrews home. He was startled from his concentration by the barking of a dog being walked by its owner. The driver of the car smiled at the lady who was glaring at the suspicious stranger in her neighborhood. He pretended that he was checking some directions as he rolled down his window.

"Excuse me but I am looking for Hammond St." He said with a thick Spanish accent.

The lady relaxed a little bit. She was familiar with that street. "You need to go about four streets that way." She said pointing in the opposite direction of Linda's house. He turned into an adjacent driveway to turn around. As he was heading in the opposite direction of Linda's house, he waved good-bye to the woman and drove off. He took on more look at Linda's house as he disappeared down the street.

At that same hour, volunteers were busy running around in the hotel conference center setting up for the opening night of the biggest event in Havocy Bay, the Writer's Symposium. The Event Coordinator, Mr. Keller, was giving out directions to the volunteers with incredible ease. He was directing them to the places that needed the most attention for the festivities that would begin in a just few hours. His British accent allowed him the benefit of the doubt with his soldiers. Anyone with a normal accent might have been misunderstood as being someone who was bossy. But with Mr. Keller, everything that flowed from his mouth came out as smooth as melted butter. It would appear that he was always the consummate gentleman.

Julian entered the hotel to check-in. As he was walking up to the counter, he gazed around checking out his surroundings. People were hustling all around him, carrying signs, tables, chairs, flowers and whatever else was deemed necessary for the event. Julian continued to walk up to the counter where a very pretty young lady was standing with a huge bright smile on her face. It was one of those smiles that automatically drew a smile from you when you encountered it. She was just finishing with a symposium attendee when Julian walked up.

"Yes sir, may I help you?"

"Hi, my name is Julian Noel and I am here to check-in."

The clerk began to pull up his information but could not find his reservation. "Sir, I cannot seem to find a reservation for you." She said apologetically.

Julian laid his hand on top of the computer monitor and said softly, "Hum, are you sure? Can you check again for me?" The clerk accommodated his request and this time she found a reservation for him.

"Sir, I am so sorry, you are right here."

"Not a problem." As the clerk was finishing up with Julian, Salomé drove up to the curbside of the hotel. A valet opened the car door for her. She got out of the car and looked around for a moment. She nodded her head in silent approval of the 5-star hotel that would be serving as her Eden while she was here to find her Pulitzer Prize winner.

Mr. Keller spotted Julian at the check-in counter and walked over to him. He extended his hand to shake Julian's. "Mr. Noel, what a great pleasure and honor it is to have you here. I am Mr. Keller the hotel manager and event coordinator."

Julian graciously accepted Mr. Keller's hand and responded, "Well, what a pleasure and honor it is to meet you."

Mr. Keller turned to the clerk. "Make sure that Mr. Noel receives whatever it is that he needs." He turned back to Julian. "And it is all on the house."

"That isn't necessary." Julian insisted.

"It isn't often that we have a guest of your importance grace this establishment. Please accept this courtesy." Julian humbly submitted to Mr. Keller's invitation. They talk for a few minutes more and a Bell Hop arrived to take Julian's bags. Julian reached into his pocket and pulled out two Fifty-dollar bills. He gave one to the clerk and the other to the Bell Hop. At the same time, he spotted Salomé entering the hotel. Julian watched her for a moment and then turned to the Bell Hop. "Can you take my bags to my room? He asked.

The Bell Hop with a big grin on his face and clutching his money replied, "Oh yes sir, right away sir." Julian nodded at the clerk, who was just as happy with her money win fall, and walked away just as Salomé walked up.

She addressed the clerk. "Hi, I am Salomé Davenport. I'm here to check-in."

"Yes, ma'am." Said the clerk as she began to pull up the information into the computer.

Julian crossed the room to a beautiful water fountain that served as the main centerpiece in the hotel lobby and stationed himself on its edge. He sat and watched Salomé check-in. He watched as she playfully tossed her hair from one shoulder to the next. He watched as the men in the hotel lobby who had gotten a glimpse of her began to fall over their feet. He noticed her pearly white teeth, the hourglass curves of her body, and the hidden scars of a heavy and wounded heart. He reached into his pocket and pulled out a pen and the notebook that he had earlier. He opened it and began to write some notes under a name already written in the book, Salomé Davenport.

6

Linda and Dorian were in the kitchen. Linda was preparing dinner and Dorian was sitting at the table with his bulking book bag. "Getting ready to practice?" Linda asked him.

Dorian unzipped his bag and pulled out a keyboard. "Not practice, but play you some tunes maybe."

Dorian played a sonata with a skill that was well beyond his age and gave evidence that he is a young music prodigy. Linda stopped what she was doing mesmerized by her son's playing. Tears began to fill her eyes. Dorian looked up and saw her crying. He detected that these were more than just tears of joy and he stopped playing.

"Mom, what's wrong? You don't like the song?"

Linda wiped her eyes feeling ashamed that she let her young son catch her in one of her emotional moments.

She walked over to him, hugged him and said, "Oh yes baby, I loved the song. I just wish that I could afford for you a real piano that's all."

"Oh come on, a real piano? I don't think that it could fit in my bag." Dorian gave her a big playful goofy smile. The one that he knew would make her laugh. He started to play T.V. tunes and singing the lyrics. Linda did laugh and sang with him as she continued to cook dinner.

The man who was in the car earlier was now standing at the fence behind Linda's house. The location gave him a perfect view of the kitchen and at the same time providing protection. He stood there a long while without being noticed. He saw a window on the side of the house near a flowerbed that was pretty well hidden from view. He pulled out a cell phone and made a call.

"Senor, there is a window on the backside of the house that is well hidden." He paused. "Si, adios." He hung up the phone and after a few moments, he walked away.

7

Salomé walked down the hall with a Bell Hop in tow carrying shopping bags. She was on her cell phone frustrated because she had been trying to get in touch with Cameron but could not reach him. She had to leave in such a hurry that she could not tell him what was going on. Salomé started talking to herself as she dialed a number on her cell phone. "You would think that a boyfriend would realize that his girlfriend is gone. He hasn't even tried to call."

"You have reached the desk of..." She hung up the phone when Cameron's voice mail came on and dialed another number.

"Hi, this is..." Again his voice mail and again she hung up the phone and dialed another number. As this was going on the Bell Hop was beginning to falter under the weight of the bags, judging from all the sweat and convulsions he was exhibiting.

"You have reached..." She grunted and hung up the phone.

"I cannot believe this man." She looked over at her aid and realized that he was having trouble with her bags. She quickly gathered herself. "Oh I am so sorry, let me unlock the door."

The Bell Hop said, "No worries ma'am," as his arms continued trembling. Salomé opened the door and to her surprise, Cameron was sitting there in a chair looking at his cell phone and laughing.

Salomé let out a scream of joy. "Cameron!" She ran over to him and they embraced and kissed. The Bell Hop put the bags down and stood there trying not to look.

Salomé stuttered through a series of questions. "When did you? – How did you? Oh my God, who let you?"

Cameron laughing at her inability to finish a thought joked, "It is a good thing you are in publishing and not journalism?" They both laughed and continued to hug.

Suddenly, Salomé pulled away angry. "Why didn't you call me?"

Cameron walked over to tip the Bell Hop. "Well, it hasn't been easy with you blowing up my phone every two seconds." The Bell Hop thanked Cameron for the tip and left. After Cameron closed the door a pillow to the face met him as he turned back to his irate girlfriend.

"I have been trying to reach you all day," said Salomé. "I had to leave in a hurry and could not talk to you before I left. You didn't even try to call me to find out where I was. I could have been dead for all you know."

Cameron ignored her words. He took her back into his arms and kissed her. She calmed down even though she was still trying to be mad.

Cameron shook his head. "Why do women always get so full of drama when it comes to the men they love?"

She tried to push away be he wouldn't let her. "Drama? Are you trying to man-splain my emotions?" She asked with an attitude.

"Woman you know that when you didn't come back to your office from your meeting with Mr. Giles, I turned into Inspector Clouseau. Marsha told me where you were. I wanted to come here and surprise you. I have some time off so…"

"So while I work you are going to play?"

"Well, I would not put it like that. I was thinking more on the lines of after you have finished working then we could play together."

A smile came over Salomé's face. "I am so glad that you are here." She said softly.

Cameron responded playfully, "I know." He plopped down on the bed and gave her a wink.

"But you are not staying in this room with me." She said sternly.

"Oh come on baby." Cameron cried out.

"No Cameron you are not staying in my room."

"Boy, you are so sure that was my intention." He removed a passkey from his pocket to a room across the hall. "What kind of a man to you take me for. I know this body is hard to resist." He flexed his non-existent muscles. "But for the sake of our commitment to God wisdom to wait, professionalism, and the Giles publishing name, get control of yourself."

Salomé picked the pillow up off of the floor and unsuccessfully chased Cameron around the room. He finally let her catch him and they fell to the floor in laughter.

8

Linda was sitting at a makeshift desk in her living room engaged in her evening ritual of writing. All around her were books on the many aspects of writing. There were also tons of journals. Only one or two of them seemed to be new. A flyer for the Writer's Symposium was also on the desk.

The discolored edges of the paper on the journals testified that she had been writing her deepest thoughts for some time. When it came to working on a manuscript, Linda was a purist - using only an old fashion typewriter. A purist maybe or it could just be the fact that she could not afford a computer and the fancy software that's used today. For whatever reason, there Linda sat at the old beat up apparatus, typing.

After awhile Dorian entered the room unnoticed. "Hey mom, what 'cha doin?"

Linda pointed to an English book and responded, "What 'cha doin?"

"Aw mom, I'm just kidding, but if it will make you feel better, I say what are you doing Mum?" He asked in his best English accent.

Linda took the piece of paper out of her pocket that she picked up off the floor earlier that day at work and threw it at him. She had not changed because her work clothes, a couple of pairs of jeans, a few tops and one dress were all she owned. The rest of her money went to keep a roof over their heads and Dorian in his private school. "You are such the wise guy." She said.

Dorian picked the paper up off the ground. He read what is written on it. "Hey mom, do you need this back? It has some writing on it but it's not your handwriting."

Linda stopped typing to go investigate the paper. "Not my handwriting?" She looked at it. "Oh my goodness. This is the piece of paper that I picked up off of the floor today at work. A customer was in there writing. He was having as much trouble as I always do."

"I don't know what you are talking about. I love reading what you write."

"I'm your mother, you have to say that."

"So do you tell me you like my playing just because I am your son?"

Linda hesitated before answering. "Don't you have some homework to do or compose a concerto or something?" Dorian laughed and picked up the flyer.

Linda read what was written on the paper out loud. *"It is only when you decide to come out of your comfort zone that you will begin to fly beyond the mortal boundaries of your existence…"*

"Sounds a little Emerson, doesn't he?" Dorian stated.

Linda shocked by her sons' keen observation replied, "Boy what do you know about Emerson?"

"Not much. Just the bits and pieces I get from, TLC, PBS, The Cartoon Network. Hey mom, why aren't you at this?" He said referring to the flyer.

"That's just for published writer's sweetie."

"You are a writer. You write every day. This does not say that you have to be a published writer. As a matter of fact, they are having a session for those who are trying to break into the business."

Linda took the flyer from him and studied it. "It doesn't say anything about that."

Dorian retorted. "Yeah well, you see they have this thing in school called the Internet." Linda gave him a look of warning to which Dorian responded to with a much more respectful tone. "Sorry. I looked up the information about the event day's ago at school when you brought the flyer home. I think you should go. There are going to be workshops and publishers there and everything."

"I see," Linda said. "It must cost an arm and a leg."

"It's only $35 at the door," Dorian told her trying to ease her mind.

"Baby, right now $35 might as well be a million. Plus I cannot leave you here by yourself."

Dorian protested. "I'm not a baby mom."

Linda responded firmly. "No, but you are too young to be left alone by yourself at night. There will be no more discussion about it."

Dorian looked at her for a moment and then left the room. Linda sat back down at her desk and continued to type. A few minutes later the doorbell rang. Linda went to the door and looked through the peephole. It was Mrs. Winder, her neighbor. She opened the door. "Mrs. Winder, what are you doing here?"

"What am I doing here? Dorian just called and said that you needed a sitter."

Linda yelled for Dorian. She walked back into the living room with Mrs. Winder. Dorian was standing there with money in his hand extended towards her.

"Dorian," Linda said his name with a touch of remorse in her voice. She saw the desire in her son's eyes for her to go but she could not tell him why she should not.

Dorian recognized that his mother was going to come up with another excuse so he cut her off. "Please, mom. Please go. Please. Here is the money and Mrs. Winder said that she would sit with me."

"Baby, I can't take your money. You work hard for this money. Raking leaves, walking dogs…"

Dorian interrupted. "Mom, this is our money."

Linda sat down on the sofa. "Dorian I just can't. I'm not ready for this kind of thing."

"Just like I felt I wasn't ready for my first recital?" Dorian questioned.

"This is not the same thing," Linda argued.

"Why isn't it dear?" Mrs. Winder interjected.

Linda was flustered by the attacks on both fronts. She continued to protest. "I just won't be comfortable."

Dorian walked over to the desk and picked up the crumpled piece of paper. He then approached his mother who was still sitting on the sofa, put his hand on her shoulder and read, *"It is only when you when you decide to come out of your comfort zone, that you will begin to fly beyond the mortal boundaries of your existence..."* He put the money into Linda's hands. Linda hugged her son so tight.

"I don't know if all mothers have received a piece of heaven from their children but I know I have." She kissed him and stood up. "Well, I guess I'm going to the Symposium."

Dorian jumped with excitement.

"Well alright!" Shouted Mrs. Winder.

9

The conference center area was buzzing and packed with would-be writers and renowned publishers from all over. Julian was signing autographs while he was getting ready for his poetry reading.   Salomé and Cameron entered the room. Mr. Keller spotted Salomé from across the room and sauntered over to where she and Cameron stood. He glanced quickly at her nametag and called out to her as if they have known each other for years. "Ms. Davenport, how are you doing this evening?" He took her hand in his and kissed it. Salomé was extremely embarrassed. She was not able to recall neither this man's name nor his face.

"I do apologize." She said. "But…"

He interjected, "Mr. Keller, hotel manager, and event coordinator. It is a pleasure to have a representative from Giles Publishing here."

Salomé was baffled as to how Mr. Keller seemed to know all about her. He saw her predicament and answered her unasked questions. "Simon Giles and I are really good friends. I talked to him earlier and he told me that you were coming." He took her hand again. Cameron's yellow-tinted skin began to show redness.

Mr. Keller continued. "I see that he has not lost his way with words. From the description he gave to me of you, there would be no way that I could mistake who you are." He kissed her hand again.

Salomé discreetly pulled it away watching Cameron turn redder every second. She thanked Mr. Keller for his compliment.

"As I said, I could not miss." He smiled at her. "And if his description did not work, your name tag would have." They both laughed, but Cameron only gave a half-laugh. Salomé quickly realized that she has not introduced her now tamale red boyfriend.

"Oh, this is my co-worker and special friend, Cameron Day." Without so much as a glance at Cameron, Mr. Keller said hello.

"Well, I must be off to make sure that everything is set for our poetry reading with Mr. Noel." He looked deeply into Salomé's eyes. "You will be there Ms. Davenport?"

Cameron answered. "Yes, we both will."

Mr. Keller responded in a snide tone glaring at Cameron. "Of course you will. Good evening." He turned and walked away.

"Can you believe that guy?" Cameron ranted throwing his hands up in the air.

"I can't believe you. You are so jealous." Salomé said grinning.

"And what the heck was that special friend crap, and why did you look like you were enjoying his drooling all over you? And I am not jealous…" Salomé just stood there letting him rant and rave, enjoying every minute of it.

Julian stood at a distance watching everything that was transpiring between Cameron and Salomé. He had his notebook out, once again - writing down notes under the pre-printed name, Cameron Day. An Aid approached to direct Julian to his place.

Linda raced through the hotel to the conference room where the poetry reading was about to start. An Aid was getting ready to close the door when he heard the voice of a woman yelling after him. It was Linda. "Wait, wait. Please wait. I have a ticket."

The Aid held the door for her. She arrived at the door out of breath and thanked the young man for excusing her tardiness. "Come on you just made it. Have a seat in the back please." Linda wouldn't have it any other way.

She walked in and was immediately blown away by all of the people that she saw. As she took her seat her attention was drawn to the stage where she saw a familiar face. "Oh my goodness. It is the man from the café." She said to herself. "The one who crumples up prolific writings and then throws them to the ground."

10

Mrs. Winder was dancing around the living room while Dorian was playing swing music on his keyboard. Mrs. Winder moved pretty well for a woman in her fifties. Her bleached blond hair swung wildly across her face. "Weeeee, play that music Dorian, play that music." Dorian laughed as he watched Mrs. Winder whirl around the room. The phone ringing interrupted them. Mrs. Winder danced over to answer it. "Hello".

"Hello, may I speak to Luminosa?" A man asked in a very heavy Spanish accent.

"To who?" Mrs. Winder questioned.

"Luminosa." The man repeated.

"I am sorry but there is no one here by that name."

"Por favor? There is no one there named Luminosa, Luminosa Andres?" The man asked as if he was pleading.

Mrs. Winder pondered and then said, "Oh my dear boy I think I see the problem. There is a Linda Andrews that lives here but not a Lumin, Lumin…"

"Luminosa." The man repeated for her.

"Yes, that name. Did you get the number from information honey?"

Across the street, a Hispanic gentleman was talking on his cell phone, looking into Linda's house. It was apparent from the expensive suit that he donned that he was a man of means. His Latin good looks were hidden behind a shadow from the tree he was standing under. A shadow had been cast from the light of a street lamp.

Carlos Andres responded deceitfully. "Information? Yes, that was it."

Mrs. Winder giggled. "I believe that they confused your Luminosa Andres with the Linda Andrews that lives here."

"Yes, I can see. In that case, tell Linda that I called for her por favor."

Mrs. Winder implored. "But I think you have..." Carlos hung up the phone. Mrs. Winder put the phone back on the hook and looked for a piece of paper - trying to make sense of the most bizarre telephone conversation. "My that was weird." She said.

Dorian who never quit playing asked, "Who was that?"

"Wrong number" Mrs. Winder responded as she wrote the message down. Dorian continued to play. Mrs. Winder resumed her dancing after she put the message that she had written on the coffee table with the name Luminosa Andres. Meanwhile, the dark Mercedes pulled up to where Carlos Andres was. He got into the car and the driver who had been in the neighborhood earlier sped away down the street.

"Is that her?" The driver of the car asked.

"Yes, with a changed name of course. Smart but not smart enough."

"Are you going to do anything tonight?"

"No, not yet, not tonight. However, I will stay close. Let me know when she is on the way." The driver nodded and pulled into a deserted parking lot except for a Silver Aston Martin. Carlos got out of the car and headed over to the vehicle. The driver of the other car left. Carlos opened the car door and got in. He pulled a cigar from his pocket, bit the end off and lit it. He rested his head against the back of his seat after taking in a long drag of the cigar - holding the smoke in his mouth for a moment and then releasing.

He reached over and opened the glove compartment and removed an envelope. He opened it and pulled out some pictures. They were baby pictures of a little boy. One was of the baby boy sitting with Carlos at a piano. Carlos stared at the picture for a long while. He began to reflect back to that night so many years ago.

Years earlier

The room was dark and foreboding and Carlos slowly entered. As he was walking through the Foyer towards the living room, he looked upstairs and saw light coming from under the door to his bedroom. He walked over to his piano. The only light was the full moon that bounced off the black lacquer of his baby grand. He takes a cigar out of his pocket and lights it. He puts it in his mouth letting it dangling from the corner. The smoke floats over a drink that was sitting there waiting for him. The Driver enters and hands Carlos some papers.

"She withdrew the money and closed the accounts. The Bank Manager assisted her. She also got the passports for her and the kid updated. Sir, she's planning on skipping town with your money and your son."

Carlos begins to speak, "It is amazing how such a beauty can be so conniving and deceitful. That such a beautiful one can turn you into a fool. Thank you, my friend."

The Driver leaves. Carlos puts the papers down and begins to play a haunting and painful melody. As he finishes playing, he extinguishes his cigar on the piano bench and then downs his waiting drink. He leaves the piano and approaches the stairway leading up to his bedroom. He slowly walks up the stairs, taking a pair of black leather gloves out of his pocket. He puts them on flexing his hands into a fist. He comes to the bedroom door and flings it open. The room is empty except for the luggage that is half full of clothes and an empty closet.

He looks around and sees no one. But he does see that balcony doors are open. He looks in horror and he races out of the room down the hall to another room. He burst through the door and rushes to a crib only to find it empty. Carlos stands trembling. He looks up and sees that the balcony doors are also open. He runs out onto the balcony and lets out howling screams that fill the night air with one word, Luminosa.

Carlos is startled into the present when ashes from his cigar fall into his lap. He quickly brushes them away and continues to look through the pictures finally stopping at one of the boy who now looked to be around 10 years old. It was Dorian Andrews.

11

Julian was sitting on the stage looking around at the crowd of hopeful would-be writers. They were there in search of any inspiration that they could find in the hopes of becoming great writers. Julian knew that some of them only cared about becoming rich or famous. Some of them only cared about the power that being an author could afford them. Still, others he knew had something in them to offer that would make a difference. These special ones had a gift to give to the world that would help to make it a better place. As he was looking out into the crowd, he saw one of those special ones – sitting in the back - trying her best to be invisible. He knew his task would be a difficult one.

The Master of Ceremony walked up on the stage. "Good evening ladies and gentlemen. Welcome to our 10th Writers by the Seaside Symposium." There was an eruption of applause from the audience. Linda looked around and became more painfully aware that a sea of people who were either writer's or wanted to become writers surrounded her. What had she been thinking? What was she, a waitress, doing here? Who was she kidding? She started to get up to leave but noticed that the attendant at the door looked like he would take offense to anyone leaving now that the program had started. Linda sank down into her seat praying that time would pass quickly.

The MC continued. "As you all know tonight is the official opening of our 3-day event and boy what a way to open it up. Tonight before you on this very stage we have the world-renowned Author and Poet, Julian Noel." Everyone jumped to their feet except Linda who eventually rose slowly so as not to bring attention to herself. She joined in the boisterous adoration, even though she had not realized that her frequent customer was a celebrity. This left her somewhat bewildered. She had never heard of this man before. She thought that she kept herself up to date on writers, especially poets since this was her favorite form of writing. Judging from the crowd's reaction, he must be something special.

The MC quieted the crowd and proceeded. "Now I have been instructed by Mr. Noel to bypass an anthology of his work. So without further ado, I present to you, Mr. Julian Noel." More handclaps, shouts, and whistles filled the hall as the crowd once again gave this man a standing ovation. Linda, now less concerned with the fact that she did not know him, was more upset that some of the titles to his work were not given. She wanted to learn more about him.

Julian stood and approached the microphone. A chair and a little glass of water were placed there as he had requested. He took his seat but ceased to look at the crowd. He studied his fingernails and took a sip of water as the crowd continued to whoop and holler. This display meant nothing to Julian. He understood that most of them did not care about him, only what they thought he could do for them. He did not want their worship. That belongs to someone else totally. He was there only to break up that fallow ground of their hearts so that their attention, talents, and desires would be directed toward the one to whom all praise was due and to be of service and healing to others.

Linda and a few others recognized that Julian was waiting for the crowd to quiet down, so they took their seats. After a few seconds, others began to follow suit until it was totally quiet in the room. The room became so quiet that you could hear a pin drop. Julian still sat there motionless. He was so deliberate with his actions. He was waiting for the precise moment when he truly had them open to receive and not just respond by rote.

Julian lowered the microphone stand and while he was seated he asked the attendee's this question. "So you want to be writers? He paused. There was no response so he asked again. "So you want to be writers?

The crowd recognized that he was asking them a direct question and they shouted out, "Yes!"

Julian continued. "So then, what you are telling me is that you have something to say. You have something that someone needs to hear. It may not be popular, or for the masses. It may only be for one person. It may not make you rich or famous, but no matter what, you have something to say."

There was a haunting silence now. Linda considered the question. She had never thought about her writing that way before. Did she have something to say? What was her reason for wanting to write? She continued to listen to Julian now with increased interest. Julian took one more sip of water, got up from his chair and came down off the stage.

He walked over to a man with stringy brown hair, outdated horned rimmed glasses on, who was about 42 years old, even though the pimples on his face made him appear as one who was in the beginning stages of puberty. He asked him directly, "You. What do you have to say?"

"Me?" The man asked.

"Yes, you." Julian answered in the tone of a high school teacher. You know the teachers who always knew the ones who were not prepared for class but called on them anyway. Julian continued. "What is it that is burning to get out of you? What is it that has to be written down for the world to read or to see on the big screen, TV or in the bathroom? What is it?

The man stared at Julian blankly and then stated, "I just want to write How-to Books."

"For what?" Julian inquired.

"To tell people how to do stuff."

"What stuff? Just any stuff? What kind of stuff are you passionate about?" Julian continued to prod.

The man shrugged his shoulders. "Nothing, in particular, I just like to write and I think 'How To' books will sell."

Julian turned away from the man walked among the people and said, "Ok then, tell me how to do something."

"What?" The man replied in shock.

Julian interjected playfully. "Oh that's right, you are a writer. Then write down how you would tell me to do something." Julian walked over to a table that had pencils and paper on it, grabbed a handful and gave them to the man.

"Now?" Said the man horrified.

"Yes now." Julian answered.

"Just like that?" The man, still in shock, questioned.

"Yes. You are a writer with something to say so write it."

The man sat there paralyzed, with pencil in hand, and just starred at the paper for a few seconds. Trying to come up with something to write but could not, he became frustrated. He could have written down several things before Julian asked if he 'really' had something to say. "It just doesn't come that easy." He said to Julian as he put the pencil down.

"No, it does not. You are right. And when you don't truly have something to say - If you are not passionate about what you are doing, it, writing, becomes even harder and lifeless. But when you do have something to say - that something that must come out or it will eat you up inside – that something that will add value to this thing called life and write it with passion - the words cannot stay imprisoned inside of you."

He walked through the crowd and looked directly at Linda, who was now hanging on his every word. He paused for a moment and then walked over to Salomé and Cameron who were in the publisher's section. He pulled up a chair and sat down between them.

"With passion, nothing can be held back." He directed the attention to Salomé and Cameron. "For instance, I hope that I am not overstepping my bounds by saying that you two are a couple."

Salomé and Cameron both blushed but do not protest and nodded their heads with a yes. Julian looked out at the crowd and asked the attendees, "Do you know how I could tell? I could see the passion that exists between them. It's their body language. I can almost hear his heart beating and the irises of her eyes are so dilated. So much passion. Someone, what else do you see between them?" The room was once again full of silence as would-be writers try to articulate what they see - if they saw anything at all.

Linda sat there looking at the couple studying them. Before she realized what was going on her mouth opened and the word flowed forth, "Magnetism."

Julian jumped up from the table excited. "Who said that?"

The people who were sitting around Linda began to point her out much to her chagrin. But not being able to contain herself she said "Magnetism. They have magnetism."

Julian began to walk carefully towards her. He did so in the same manner that one approaches an animal that you are trying not to spook. "Magnetism. What a passionate word. Why did you choose that one?"

Linda swallowed hard. "It's what I see in them. It's all over them."

Julian turned back to the crowd but does not move too far away from Linda. "Vision - the ability of the writer to perceive and see the ethereal all around him or her."

Julian explained what ethereal meant. "That unseen reality which gives birth to that which we do see. It is the inner ability to know that something greater exists beyond ourselves. It is that invisible something that gives us evidence of the Divine. You can find it within the pulse of your wrist, the flight of birds, the gentle breeze of the wind on your skin. It is this ethereal that the poets, painters, musicians, or your grandpa explaining the tides of the ocean waves, give expression to. To be able to articulate the existence of this unseen in writing is a gift from the Divine."

Julian continued. "It is this vision that enables you to unlock the prison doors of those words locked away. It is this vision that allows you to write at a drop of a hat."

The man whom Julian called on earlier raised his hand and asked this question? "What does that vision have to do with writing 'How to' books?"

"Without the vision of the Divine, who gives us the desire to help one another, your endeavor becomes selfish and self-centered. All such activity undertaken with such motives is destined to become empty and will cause your writing to be ineffective." The man wanted to say one thing in response to that statement but Julian interrupted him. "Even if you are not trying to change the world." The man dropped his head and allowed Julian to continue. Julian walked back to the stage. "Well thanks to Ms. Davenport, Mr. Day and Ms. Andrews, we have our first practice example of having something to say in our writing." The three of them looked mystified that he was able to call their names out, but Salomé was more interested as to what part she played in providing such an example.

"We do?" She asked in a way that drew much laughter from the crowd.

"Yes, we do," Julian responded with some laughter of his own. "We have love and magnetic passion. No better subject to write about." He turned in the direction of Linda. "Ms. Andrews, will you please join me up here?"

Linda looked up at Julian like she was a deer with her eyes caught in headlights. She managed to mumble, "You want me to join you up there?"

Julian softly answered but in no uncertain terms, "Yes ma'am. This symposium is more than just a lecture session - it is a writing clinic. So, therefore, someone, like you, will have to write."

Linda slowly got out of her seat thinking of how many different ways she was going to yell at her son when she got home.

As she was walking up, she did not realize that she was verbalizing some of her thoughts until she heard Julian's question. "Did you say something, Ms. Andrew?"

Linda stopped walking at his question turned and looked at the door, while answering, "No."

Julian noticed that his pupil was looking at the door trying to calculate how difficult it would be just to run out. That was exactly what Linda was thinking. She would just run out. Run back to her little four-room house with one bathroom. Run back to her dead-end thankless waitress job. Run back to her beat-up old typewriter. What difference would it make? She was used to running. She was just about to turn and leave when she heard Julian speak to her. It stopped her cold. She could not move towards the door. There was something in his voice as he directed his words toward her. She could not explain it but those words unlike any that he had spoken that night reached out to her. Reached out for her. She knew that somehow she was the only one that heard them.

"False comfort maybe out there Ms. Andrews but your dreams are up here."

Julian let it stand at that. He said nothing else. It was up to her now. Linda looked at the door one more time then turned and started to walk towards the stage. Julian reached for her hand. It had been a long time since a man had used his hands to help her. As she stood on the stage Julian whispered in her ear, "It's time to unlock those words. It's time to unlock the passion."

Linda felt a strange calm come over her. Julian escorted Linda to a blackboard that had been brought onto the stage. The sight touched Salomé looking on. Somehow she could feel the fear but the need to overcome that Linda was feeling. How many times was she in the same position at Harvard – trying to prove that she was someone - that she mattered. She did not know Linda but she knew Linda.

Julian began to address the crowd. "Ok. Ms. Andrews and I are going to write a poem about Ms. Davenport and Mr. Day." He turned to Linda. "Ms. Andrews, I want you to study the two of them while I start the poem. I will start it off but you will finish it. Ok?"

Linda responded nervously. "Ok."

"We'll call it Magnetism, cool?"

"Cool," Linda answered back trying to crack a smile.

Julian comforted her. "Don't worry. Just let it flow. Believe me, it is in there. I know it. Now you must know it and just let it flow." Linda turned back and looked at Salomé and Cameron for a moment. She then closed her eyes. She opened them again and the room seemed to have turned into a tunnel. She could no longer see the people around her. All of a sudden, words burst into the air and began to flow around in the room in vibrant colors. She began picking them out of the air one by one and placed them in her mind in the right places just as an artist does with paint on his canvas.

Julian touched her shoulder asking if she was ready and then handed her the chalk. Linda without hesitation took the chalk and began to write where Julian left off on the board. She had not noticed that Julian had only written one word on the board, Magnetism. Linda wrote with a fervency of a person whose very life depended on it. She finally finished in a span of a few moments but Linda felt like she had entered a realm of the eternal. She did not want to look at what she had written. She felt that she must have left her much-hidden soul on that board. Linda handed the chalk back to Julian and stood to the side.

Julian read over the poem, looked over at Linda in amazement and then began to read it out loud.

Magnetism

He says *– I cannot resist you, lady, no matter how hard I try. The force to which this is due lies behind your piercing eyes. I enter your presence and in my magnetic pole, this force begins to concentrate. In those magnetic* *moments, I get dizzy, I lose all common sense, not able to think straight.*

She says *- I try to deny it but your soul sends out to me undeniable electric signals, magnetically recording on my heart - this magnetic pick-up of soul mates that should never part.*

They say *- Magnetism leads us to a love beyond the sphere of the physical. It leads us to a place of complexity. And all that can be said is that in this magnetic field, our love, forever as one, shall be."*

There was a short moment of continued silence from a crowd that sat mesmerized. But soon the silence was broken with claps that expand into loud applause. Julian who had joined in with the crowd clapping shouted, "Now that is what I call unlocking the words!"

Linda realized that the merriment she heard was for her. Suddenly flashbulbs started going off all around her. Reporters at the event began to take pictures of her. Mr. Keller was now on the stage making sure that he got in on the pictures. Linda started to get frantic. With every flash of a bulb or the clicking of a camera shutter, she became more frightened.

"Excuse me please but I need to get back to my seat." Linda pleaded with the throngs of reporters trying to get a picture. Mr. Keller grabbed onto her. "Come on now, you don't want to miss your moment of glory do you?"

The MC took the stage beside Mr. Keller and Linda. "Well, it looks like the contest has started early."

"Contest? What contest?" Linda asked.

The MC began to explain. "We have invited publishers from all over to come and experience the writing talent that we bring together. There is a $50,000.00 writing contract on the table. We only invite the best and the brightest of writing talent to enter, people who have had some type of publishing exposure."

Julian, who had been keeping his eye on Linda since the camera's started flashing, began to inch his way towards her. The MC continued. "Fate, however, drops us pleasant surprises from time to time."

Julian who had reached Linda to comfort her interjects a response to the statement just made by the MC.

"Fate, not hardly, Divine intervention maybe, but never fate." Julian smiled at Linda who was looking up at him and then he whispered in her ear, "Are you ready to go?" Linda nodded discreetly and the crowd which could not be moved early by Linda's pleas, separated, opening up to let them through. The reporters continued to take pictures as if they did not recognize that Linda had left the stage. As she and Julian reached the exit, Salomé and Cameron approached them.

"Ms. Andrews," Salomé exclaimed, "I must say you are pure virgin talent. With a little grooming, you could become a New York list bestseller. I'm sorry you know my name but what you don't know is that I am the Jr. Editor for Giles Publishing. I would love…."

Linda cut her off. "Please Ms. Davenport. I don't mean to be rude but I have a son to get home to. It's late."

"Yes I understand, but will you be here for the rest of the events?"

"I haven't thought about it," Linda responded annoyed. The only thing that she had thought about for the last few minutes was getting the heck out of there. "Please excuse me." Linda ran out leaving them standing there.

"Wow, talk about stage fright, camera-shy, looking a gift horse in the mouth." Cameron huffed. Julian stepped up, startling them. They had not noticed him there when they were talking to Linda.

"Be patient. Fear is a debilitating force and those who suffer from it are too easily judged by other's who don't." Julian turned and left.

Cameron was standing there trying to figure Julian out. After a moment of pondering, he looked at Salomé and asked, "Who is that guy? I have never heard of him have you?"

Salomé was not listening to Cameron's questions. She was only thinking about the woman who had so brilliantly written down how she knew she and Cameron felt about one another. She looked over at Cameron, bright-eyed and bushy-tailed. "We have to find that woman. Mr. Giles, I found that Pulitzer Prize winner!"

12

Linda ran through the hotel with only one thought in mind – to find the nearest exit. Julian was running after her. He was about to catch her when his notebook fell out of his pocket. It fell open as it hit the ground with the word 'STOP' printed in it. He ceased his pursuit and helplessly watched as Linda exited the hotel. It would not be for him to talk to her anymore that night.

Linda finally reached the bus stop and clasped on the waiting bench. She closed her eyes as she tried to catch her breath while she waited for the bus. She mused over what had just transpired. Were they really clapping for her? Was that a real publisher who wanted to talk to her about her writing?

"Why did you run away? Why are you always running away?" She said to herself. She closes her eyes and thinks back.

Ten years earlier

Linda is frantically running around an elaborately decorated bedroom throwing as many clothes into a suitcase as possible. The ceiling light is dancing off of the 3-carat princess cut ring on her finger, sending rainbow shimmers all around the room. She freezes as she hears a door open and the echo of footsteps coming from downstairs. She stands motionless. Her chest begins to heave as her breathing becomes erratic. Linda whispers to herself, "He's home too soon." She stops her packing and slowly heads toward the balcony doors of the bedroom.

Her musing was broken up by the sound of a grumpy hoarse voice of a man. "Hey, are you getting on or what?" Linda looked at the man through the open doors of the bus and remembered that she is going home. She got on to the bus but forgot to pay her fare.

The bus driver, who appeared to have driven to one too many stops, reminded her. "Hey, do you think that this is your private limo or something lady?" She looked at the bus driver pointing to the fare amount sign. She reached for her bus pass and ran it through the meter. She then found an empty seat and collapsed in it. She looked around at the people on the bus staring at their empty faces. She pondered over the words that Julian had spoken earlier. Did she have something to say - to write for these poor souls on the bus that could make their lives better? She laughed to herself. "Yeah, they really want to hear from someone who has to use a bus pass."

As the bus pulled away, the Mercedes that had been in Linda's neighborhood earlier and had been driving around Carlos Andres was parked across the street from the hotel. The driver pulled off as the bus was leaving but went in a different direction. The driver of the car pulled out his cell phone and made a call. The phone rang and he waited for an answer on the other end. "She is on the way. Understood." He hung up the phone and sped down the street making a sharp right turn almost on two wheels, driving out of sight.

The bus Linda was on pulled into her neighborhood. She tiredly tugged the cord to let the bus driver know to let her off. She was extremely tired now. Standing all day on her feet and the emotional toll of what had taken place at the symposium left her drained. Her thank-you and goodnight to the bus driver were only met with a grunt and a thump of the doors closing behind her as she stepped off the bus.

Linda started walking toward her home. A man hidden in the shadows followed slowly behind. Linda sensed that someone was behind her turned around slowly to look but saw no one. She continued to walk down the street and the man continued to follow. Linda sped up but looked back over her shoulder again as she heard slow methodical footsteps behind her. She saw something in the shadows but could not make it out. She continued to focus trying to make out the figure.

All of a sudden there was a crashing sound behind her. Linda whirled back around screaming. One of her neighbors Homer, knocked over some of his trashcans as Linda was walking up. "Sorry, Linda, having a clumsy moment. I didn't mean to scare you."

Linda was breathing heavily but glad to see Homer responded, "No problem. I just have to find my heart and put it back in my chest." Pointing to the ground playfully, "Oh there it is!" They both laugh as Linda helped Homer pick up his cans.

"Well at least let me make up for it by walking you to your door." He said to Linda extending his arm.

Linda puts her arm through his. "Please do." They strike up some small talk. Linda looked back behind her but saw nothing. She said thank-you and good night to Homer. He gestured as if he would be tipping his hat if he had on one and headed back to his house. Linda looked one more time unlocked the door and went into the house. She could not see from her angle, in the shadows, glimmering in the light from a lamppost, the blade of a knife in the hand of a gloved man.

13

Mrs. Winder was asleep in a chair when Linda walked into the house. Linda smiled to herself as she listened to a resonating snore coming from the sleeping babysitter. Linda was careful to walk over to her to wake her up. "Mrs. Winder, Mrs. Winder," Linda called out.

Mrs. Winder woke up as if she had not been sleeping. "Why hello dear. Oh my goodness you are back. What time is it?" Linda turned to look at the clock that was ticking rhythmically on the mantel.

"It's about 11:30," Linda said as she was pulling off her shoes to the welcomed relief of her feet. "Did everything go ok around here tonight?" Linda asked.

"Oh yes. Dorian and I had a marvelous time tonight. What about you dear?" Mrs. Winder asked looking for some juicy details.

Linda smiled as she answered, "Well I have to admit it went pretty well." Mrs. Winder started to gather her things with sleep returning to her bloodshot eyes.

"You know, your son knew that would be the case. He is your biggest fan. I believe if he sees you do something with your writing, there is nothing that he won't be able to do."

Linda pondered what she had just heard. "You think that I have that kind of effect on him?"

"All parents do dear." Mrs. Winder said in a heartening way. "He is right you know."

"Right about what?" Linda asked.

"You are a great writer. I took a little peak."

"Oh you did, did you?" Linda said lightheartedly. Mrs. Winder grinned bashfully. She remembered the message that she had taken earlier and was getting ready to tell Linda about it when a sleepy Dorian walked into the room.

"Mommy." He called out to Linda in a voice that reminded her, that no matter how talented he was or how much she told her that he was not a little man but a man, he was still so dependent on her. Linda walked over to him.

"Hi, baby. What are you doing out of bed?"

"I was waiting up for you." He said with a yawn. Linda took him by the hand and led him to his bedroom. Mrs. Winder had gathered her things together and had accidentally put a magazine on top of the message that someone called for Luminosa Andres. She did not think much of it since she felt that the gentleman had the wrong number anyway. She walked out of the house and locked the door. She figured that Linda would see the note.

Dorian was still asking his mother questions, even though he was falling back asleep. "Did you meet any writers?"

"Yes." She said as she got him back in bed. In his room were collections of posters with some of the greatest musicians that ever lived and were living. Linda also had a mural painted on the wall of a classical pianist playing in a grand hall.

Dorian continued with his inquiry. "Were they famous?"

"One was," Linda answered as she pulled the covers over him.

"Did you show him any of your writings?" Dorian asked.

"Well, as a matter of fact, I did," Linda told him lying down beside him.

Dorian yawned again and his eyes closed but he asked one more question. "Did he like it?"

Linda smiled and answered, "Yes. A lot of people did."

Dorian was able to muster one more response before he fell completely asleep again. "Smart people." Linda smiled at the little angel lying there in his bed. She leaned over and kissed him gently on the cheek and propped herself up on a pillow and fell asleep herself.

Outside of Dorian's window, the moonlight cast a silhouette shadow of the trees across the peaceful sleeping mother and son. An ominous presence disturbed this picture as a moving shadow of a man passed over the unsuspecting pair. The shadow became stationary as the man stared through the window. He took the knife that was in his hand and rubbed the blade across his face. Small flakes of paint fell to the ground as the blade rubbed against the roughness of his visage.

Something tripped a motion sensor detector of a neighbor of Linda's house, shining a light directly on the man. It flashed like lightning clearly exposing Carlos Andres's face. The flash of light caused him to run away. The bright light shining through the window woke Linda up. She sat up in the bed in a hurry. She heard the sound of running footsteps. She slowly got out of the bed keeping low and walked over to the window. She slowly pulled the curtains back and saw a neighborhood dog digging around in the yard. She let out a sigh and crawled back in bed with Dorian.

Carlos had gotten back into his car that he had parked a couple of blocks away. As he drove away a cry of sadness from the ocean whales could be heard in the distance.

14

It was Saturday morning and Cameron was deep in sleep. From the look on his face, he was having a wonderful dream when he was shocked out of it by the sound of the alarm clock going off. At the same time, Salomé was knocking crazily on Cameron's hotel door. Cameron reached over and turned off the alarm. He sat up in the bed shaking the cobwebs out of his head. "I'm coming, I'm coming." He yelled. He shuffled his feet across the floor as he went to open the door.

As he opened the door, Salomé rushed past him. "Good morning sweetheart." She danced through the room turning on the lights. She went through Cameron's suitcase looking for some clothes.

Cameron, who could barely keep his eyes open, stumbled to the bathroom. "Good morning? Woman are you crazy? It's only 6 a.m. Wait. Did you set my clock for this early?"

"Yes, and we are losing daylight. So come on get ready and let's go." She tossed some mix-matched clothes in his direction.

"Losing daylight? What daylight? It's still dark out." He turned and started to walk back to the bed. Salomé rushed behind him with the shirt that she picked out and started putting it on him.

"Cameron we have to go and find that woman."

"What woman?" Cameron asked, taking the shirt off.

Salomé jumped on the bed. As she was jumping up and down she responded, "Linda Andrews. I have already called Mr. Giles. He will be here tomorrow. We have to find her and get her to sign with Giles Publishing."

Cameron, who sat on the bed bouncing up and down as Salomé continued to jump asked, "You believe that she can be that good?"

"I believe she is that good." She jumped off the bed and composed herself. "Come on get dressed and let's go."

Cameron looked at his girlfriend and wondered if she had completely lost her mind. Did she feel that this woman Linda was good enough or was the pressure of 3 bad reviews getting to her? No matter what, he was there to support her. "Where do you think that we are going to find this woman?"

Salomé who was walking towards the door stopped as she put her hand on the doorknob. She turned looked at Cameron with those beautiful doe-like chestnut eyes and answered, "I have no idea." She opened the door and left his room.

Cameron started to put on the clothes but then glanced at the clock. "6:07, she's got to be kidding me." He fell backward on the bed pulling his blanket over his head.

Dorian bolted out of the front door and started running down the street with his bulging backpack in tow. Linda came to the door and stood on the porch yelling after him. "Dorian, don't forget that I will be at the symposium tonight. Mrs. Winder will be here after you get home from piano practice."

Dorian yelled back. "Gotcha mom!" He continued to run down the street. Linda stepped off of the porch. It was the time of day that she watered her flowers that she had planted in a little makeshift garden on the side of her house. She grabbed the hose humming a little melody to herself. She felt something gritty on her hands and noticed that the hose had more dirt on it than normal. She thought this unusual because she kept the hose off the ground.

She looked around and found that there has been some disturbance around her flowers. "That's weird." She said to herself. She studied what looked like footprints but she could not quite make them out as such. A barking dog pulled her attention away. It was Mr. Lee and his dog. Linda remembered the dog being in her yard the night before. Mr. Lee waved to Linda and said good morning.

Linda waved back and said, "Good morning Mr. Lee and Hugo." She started to water her flowers and cease her investigation. She muttered under her breath. "Dumb dog messing up my flowers." Linda finished watering her flowers and returned the hose to its rightful place. She gazed upon her flowers one more time pleased with her blossoms and went back inside. She failed to notice the broken flakes of paint that had fallen from her window seal and that a slit had been cut into it and the lock pried up.

15

Salomé and Cameron were in the lobby of the hotel talking to the aid that worked the night before at the poetry reading/clinic. "We just need a little information from you," Salomé said with a flirtatious smile on her face.

"What kind of information?" The aid responded with little interest in Salomé's smile.

She responded. "I need some information on the young lady that wrote with Mr. Noel last night. I need her contact info."

"I'm sorry; I cannot give that information out."

"Oh, why not?" Salomé asked coyly.

"That information is private." He responded somewhat annoyed.

Cameron chimed in. "She was here for the writer's symposium. Most likely wanting to become a writer." He said with a sardonic tone. He continued. "We work for a publishing company. Writer – publishing company. Get my drift?"

"Yes." The aid answered back unmoved by Cameron's wit.

"Good. Then we understand each other."

The aid smiled and said, "I understand you, but you don't understand me. I can't give you the information that you are looking for." Salomé and Cameron were going to protest again but the aid interrupted them. "Look, she will be here according to her registration card. So just wait for her to show up." He paused. "Like the rest of the publishing professionals."

Cameron flexed. "Are you trying to get funny with us?"

Salomé stepped in. "Cameron, calm down. This fine young man is just doing his job. Never mind that he might cause an aspiring writer to miss out on an opportunity of a lifetime."

The aid rolled his eyes at her. "Please, Ma'am. Do not think that just because I am sitting behind this table, that I am ignorant and gullible. I hold a Master's in Psychology. So that reverse jazz won't work on me."

Cameron tired of the dance pulled a hundred dollar bill out of his pocket and waved it at the aid. "What about the greenbacks and all that jazz?"

The aid took the money and said, "Hatch, whoopi, and all that jazz, ha, ha, ha." Salomé looked at him crazily.

"That is a line from the musical All that Jazz," Cameron told her. The aid pulled the card with Linda's information on it but he does not let go of it. Cameron bellowed. "Hey man, release please."

The aid refused. He told them, "I'll let you write down the information but I will not let you take the card. I do operate with some discretion."

Salomé and Cameron just look at each other. "It's not worth it. Just write the information down before you have to come to bail me out of jail." Cameron said. Salomé took out her phone and took a picture of the information. They both half-heartedly thanked the aid and ran out of the hotel.

As Salomé and Cameron drove off, they did not see Linda getting off of the bus. Linda stopped short of going into the hotel. "Come on girl. Go in. Stop being afraid." She said talking to herself. She summoned the courage and walked into the hotel. There were writers and publishers all over the place. Conversations were going on that Linda could not interpret. She could but the sight of all of those people was overwhelming her.

She watched as the authors were showing each other their published books and articles. She felt so out of place. But it started to go downhill for her when an attendee approached her from the night before.

"Hey." He called out to her. "You're Linda Andrews, the writer from lasts night clinic with Mr. Noel. Say you are great. I write short stories. I have had 10 published so far. Where have you been published?"

Linda's heart sank into her stomach with that question. The courage she had gained to walk into the hotel was lost in a wave of inferiority that caused Linda to bolt from the hotel lobby leaving the writer dazed and confused. She ran towards the beach in tears.

16

Cameron and Salomé were driving around trying to find the café where Linda worked. If it were not for the fact that their surroundings where so beautiful, it would have been a most miserable search. They passed street after street not being able to find the one they were looking for.

Cameron yelled to Salomé that she had just missed their turn. "That was where we were supposed to turn."

"Now you tell me. Can you please try and tell me a little sooner?"

"Well excuse me." Cameron snapped. "I guess you know this area like the back of your hand." Suddenly he yelled again. "Turn there!"

Salomé made a sharp left turn that caused the tires on the car to smoke and squeal.

"Why here?" Salomé asked as she gained control of the car.

"So we can turn around maybe," Cameron said.

Salomé, who ignored his smart-alecky remark asked, "Look, what is the name of the street?"

"Bull Street." He answered. "And you just passed it again." They kept driving and ended up on a one-way street.

"Was this on the map?" Asked Salomé.

Cameron glanced at her like she had lost it. "Map? What map? There's no map just the half baked directions we received from the gas station attendant. What kind of town is this with no GPS service?" As they continued to drive down the one-way street, Salomé began to recognize the surroundings.

"I recognize this area." She said. "I have been through here before."

"You have, when?" Cameron asked. Salomé looked up just as she is getting ready to answer and realized why the place was so familiar. The sign of Sea Side car rental came into her view.

Cameron instructed her, "Turn in here. I'll ask these people for directions.

Salomé laughed. "Good luck. See you in about an hour." Cameron wondered why she would make such a statement. He let it slide and went inside the building. Ravi was on the phone talking when Cameron walked in.

Ravi looked up at Cameron. "Hey, man be right with you." He returned to his customer on the phone. "Now we have…"

Outside Salomé rested her head on the back of her seat and let out a deep sigh.

17

Linda was sitting on the beach gathering herself from her self-inflicted emotional breakdown. She wondered how long she was going to allow herself to stay so afraid. Julian had been sitting there for some time now watching Linda and writing. He stopped when he saw Linda pounding her fist into the sand. He got up and walked over to her and handed her the piece of paper that he had been writing on.

"Here," Julian said.

Linda jumped. She did not realize that anyone had been on the beach with her. "What is this?" She asked Julian as she took the paper from his hand.

"It's a portrait of you," Julian replied.

Linda looked at the paper confused. "A portrait, there are only words on this paper, not a picture."

"So you are saying that words can't paint a picture?" Julian asked with a Cheshire cat smirk on his face. He knew where he was going with his question.

Linda defiantly answered. "No, they can't. Words can express what you can see but they are not a picture." She folded the paper and put it in her pocket without reading it.

Julian looked out over the ocean and the sky and said, "Well somebody forgot to send that memo to God."

"What do you mean?" Linda asked curiously.

"The memo about words not being able to paint a picture." Julian elucidated.

"So you are saying that they do?"

"Of course," Julian said pointing out their surroundings. "Look all around you. Have you ever seen a picture prettier than the one you are looking at now?"

Linda gazed out at the ocean and the clouds and the sand. "No, I guess I have not." She answered.

"God painted this with His words. Words sometimes can be the only paint that will give us an accurate picture."

Linda looked at Julian blinking. "Are you a philosopher or something? Because you don't talk like any of the people I know."

"No," Julian answered. "Just an observer. Philosophers like to talk about things without necessarily coming to a point."

"Is there a point to anything?" Linda asked.

"Yeah, living is the point," Julian replied.

18

In another part of Havocy Bay, Dorian was in school for his Saturday piano practice. His teacher was very excited over his playing. "Yes, yes Dorian, play it, play it, my boy." Exclaimed Mr. Bachzart.

An announcement came over the intercom and interrupted the session. "Mr. Bachzart, can you come to the office please?" The secretary said.

"Ahy Chi wowa. Dorian, practice your scales until I return," said Mr. Bachzart.

"Ah man, Mr. Bachzart, the scales?" Dorian complained.

Mr. Bachzart looked sternly at Dorian and said, "We have discussed this, no matter how great you are or are going to become, you must always keep your foundation strong."

Dorian rolled his eyes and began to play an elementary level scale. Mr. Bachzart started swinging his pencil like a music conductor and said, "Good, now continue to play that until I return." Mr. Bachzart exited the room. Dorian waited for a moment and then began to play the boogie-woogie. He did not notice that Carlos Andres had entered the classroom.

Meanwhile, Cameron exited the car rental shop with a dazed look on his face. Salomé looked at him and grinned. "So did you get the directions?"

Cameron handed her a piece of paper with the directions on it. His hands were shaking as he stammered, "Yes, but I have never."

Salomé leaned over and kissed him on the cheek and said, "Its ok baby, this convertible will make it all better."

At that moment, Ravi came running out of the shop. Cameron got a crazed look in his eyes and yelled to Salome', "Drive, drive, get us out of here!" Salomé sped off leaving Ravi with a big smile on his face and waving goodbye.

Salomé and Cameron finally reached Linda's place of work. They entered the quaint little coffee shop to the sound of the cook hollering, "Fried egg sandwich up!"

Salome' jumped as the cook dinged the bell. They walked up to an employee and asked for the manager. She pointed to the cook. Salomé walked up to the cook and got his attention. "Excuse me, sir." Cameron walked over to the pastry dish to partake.

The cook responded. "What'll ya have?"

"Some information please. I'm looking for Linda Andrews," Salomé said.

"Not here today. At some conference. Betty, over there is a pretty good waitress. She'll be happy to take care of you."

"No, it's business."

"She'll be back in the day after tomorrow." The cook said.

"Thank you but if I don't talk to her before then, it will most likely be too late," Salomé said as she looked around for Cameron. After she spotted him she gave the cook a 20-dollar bill thanked him and walked towards Cameron.

"Wow," said the cook. "All of a sudden Linda is a hot commodity. Some other people were in here looking for her earlier."

"Shoot," Salomé replied. "Cameron, we'll have to hurry."

She grabbed Cameron just as he was taking a bite of his second pastry. He fussed. "Chewing, chewing here!"

"We have to go. Someone else is trying to beat us to the punch."

They both ran out of the coffee shop. Jelly dripped onto Cameron's shirt from the pastry he had in his hand as Salomé pulled on him to hurriedly get to the car.

As they were both getting into the car, Cameron said, "Sal, all of this chasing and running might be a moot point."

"What do you mean?" Salomé responded as she started the car.

"We cannot sign anyone who enters or wins the contest."

Salomé turned out of the parking lot and began to drive down the street. "She never said that she would enter the contest, she said she would think about it. We just have to get to her first and offer her a sweeter deal."

"That would be great but where is she?" Cameron said throwing his hands up in the air.

"The cook said that she took off for a conference so most likely she's at the hotel."

"Guess we should have waited around like the aid said."

"And I guess you could have saved your 100 dollars."

"Not to mention my sanity that Ravi took."

They both laughed. Cameron continued. "Let's just go find her and sign her up." They speeded down the highway heading back to the hotel.

19

Linda and Julian were still walking down the beach talking. "Living huh? That's the point?" Linda asked.

"That's right," Julian said.

"Some people don't think so."

"Yeah, I know. Are you one of them?" Julian asked her.

Linda glanced at him but did not respond quickly. "I guess to answer that I will borrow a couple of lines from Sam Cook. It's been too hard living but I'm afraid to die…"

"Is that your fear, dying?"

Linda responded sheepishly. "Sometimes."

Julian said, "You know you waste a lot of valuable time thinking about death instead of living."

"Well, maybe I have a good reason to think about it."

Julian giggled. "Only if someone is after you."

Linda stayed silent.

Julian, knowing that she was deliberately avoiding his statement said, "Well, I cannot speak to that but I know that you have a very good reason for living. Your son."

Linda looked at him inquisitively and said, "How do you know about my son?"

"You mentioned him last night."

"Oh yeah," she said. "And you are right; he is my reason for living. He is my reason for a lot of things. I will do anything to keep him safe. To make sure that his life won't be so hard."

She stopped walking and turned to Julian. She looked him square in the eye and continued. "I will do anything to protect him." She proceeded walking along the beach.

Back in the music room, Dorian was still playing his boogie-woogie. Carlos called out to him from the back of the room. "You are a very good player amigo."

Dorian, startled, turned to see who was addressing him. Seeing a stranger, he reluctantly answered, "Thank you."

Carlos moved closer to where Dorian was seated. "Who taught you how to play?"

Dorian did not make eye contact with Carlos, but answered, "Nobody really. I just started playing one day and then my mom signed me up for lessons."

"Tu Madre?" Carlos asked.

"What?" Dorian replied.

"Your mother," Carlos answered in English.

"Yes," Dorian said. "She told me that God had given me a very special talent and that I should do everything to develop it and bless the world with it."

Carlos slowly stepped up to the piano. Dorian was feeling a little nervous about being alone in a room with a stranger. He looked around for Mr. Bachzart.

Carlos recognized that Dorian was uncomfortable tried to put him at ease. He asked, "May I play?"

Dorian, curious said to Carlos, "Sure."

Carlos sat down and began to play a song, that song he played all those years ago. It had Dorian sitting on the edge of his seat.

"Wow, Mr. You're great. What is that you are playing?"

Carlos looked at Dorian with tenderness in his eyes and said, "It is my own composition."

Dorian sat and watched Carlos' hand positions move effortlessly up and down the piano. As he was still playing he asked Dorian this question. "So God gave you this gift to bless the world, what about making money?"

Dorian pondered what Carlos had said and then responded, "I don't know. Guess helping people is more important."

"Oh really?" Carlos retorted. "Is that what she taught you?"

"No, that is what she has shown me. She shows me that things can get hard sometimes, but if you spend your life doing things to make others happy, to make their lives better, things will work out for you."

Carlos stopped playing and looked at Dorian. "Such innocence amigo. That is because you are so young. Are you sure this is what she practices, doing things to make other people happy?"

"Yeah!" Dorian exclaimed in a tone that reflected disbelief in the fact that this man could have even questioned it.

Carlos still looking at him paused and then asked him, "Is that what your daddy teaches you as well?"

Dorian dropped his head. "My dad is dead. He died when I was a baby. I never knew him."

Carlos clenched his fist to keep his emotions in tack. "That is too bad. All little boys should know their padres."

Dorian frowns at the wording so Carlos changed and said, "Their fathers. Dads prepare you for the world, while moms try to shield you from it."

"What do you mean?" Dorian asked.

"Let me give you an example. What your mother told you is true but only partially true. She's not trying to lie to you but she thinks she is protecting you."

"Protecting me from what?"

"The true realities of the world. See even though what she is teaching you is ideal, it is not the way the true world works." He put his hand on Dorian's shoulder. "I like you amigo, so I'm going to tell you something my father told me. You can do all you can for people and they will still break your heart. So in the real world, do whatever you can but make sure you get as much out of it for yourself as possible."

Dorian questioned, "Isn't that selfish?"

"More like survival," Carlos replied. "If you don't protect yourself, someone may come and steal from you the most precious thing in the world to you."

Dorian pondered. "But isn't it the fear of losing something that causes people to go into survival mode in the first place? Life is more than about survival. It's about loving."

Carlos was stunned by what Dorian had just said and asked, "How old are you, amigo? Only 10 right?"

"Yes, how did you know?"

"I'm a good guesser." Replied Carlos. "How does one your age bring forth such heavy insights?"

"They don't seem heavy to me. More like common sense." Dorian said.

Carlos added, "Out of the mouth of babes yes? You mention loving. A strong force. You will learn someday that love will drive people to do things that seem like anything but common sense." He smiled at Dorian as he watched him assimilate the comment he just made.

Dorian asked him, "Can you play some more?"

"Here I will show you a few bars," Carlos answered.

Dorian copied note for note what Carlos played. They laugh together as they play. All of a sudden the alarm on Carlos's watch started to beep.

Carlos looked at his watch and said, "Sorry mi amigo, but I must be going now."

"Awe man do you have to?" Dorian cried.

"Si, my young friend," Carlos answered.

"You know my mom would kill me if she knew I was talking to a stranger."

Carlos stood up to leave and replied, "She is right about that but I think that our music puts us on common ground."

He playfully ran his hand through Dorian's hair and started to leave the classroom.

Dorian stood up and yelled after Carlos. "Hey mister, I'm going to learn to play your song."

Carlos turned around to face Dorian. "I have no doubt. Adios."

Dorian replied, "Adios."

After Carlos left the classroom, Mr. Bachzart returned. Dorian was trying to play the song that he heard Carlos play. Mr. Bachzart chastised, "Dorian, those are not the scales."

"Ah, man," Dorian complained. Dorian began to play the scales again. Outside of the school building, Carlos was walking away with tears in his eyes.

<h1 style="text-align:center">20</h1>

Julian rolled up his pants legs and was walking in the ocean water. The foam from the waves covered his feet. Julian played with the sand in between his toes. He continued his conversation with Linda. "You will do anything to protect him?" That sounds a little more ominous than just a parent trying to protect their child from a boo-boo."

Linda was standing a little off from Julian said, "Once again, maybe some people have more fear than just their child receiving a boo-boo."

"Maybe. But we can no more control those situations any more than we can control if they fall and get a boo-boo." Julian was now kicking the water up in the air. He turned slightly in Linda's direction and kicked but acted as if he did not mean for the water to go her way. Linda licked her lips as a droplet of water landed on them. She grimaced at the taste of the salt.

She responded to Julian. "Yeah, but boo-boo's..." She stopped her statement short of completion realizing that their conversation was becoming ridiculous. Getting angry, she turned away from Julian and started to walk down the beach. "What are we talking about? Why are we talking about this? Why are you prodding me? You don't know me."

Julian was attempting to get Linda to break down the walls that have her imprisoned, so he kept pushing. "Do you know yourself?"

Linda stepped in the water and kicked it up at Julian. "Will you please stop with all this psycho-babble stuff? Why are you picking on me?"

"What are you hiding from?" He asked.

Linda stuttered but said forcefully, "Who says I'm hiding from anything?"

"You do." Julian snapped. "By the way you act. By your posture. By how uncomfortable you are around people."

"Well, maybe I'm just shy." Linda retorted.

"That's bull and you know it."

Linda looked at Julian with tears beginning to fill her eyes. She knew that he was right but she did not want to admit it. "I don't have to answer to you or explain my actions to you."

"No, you don't," Julian said. "But you will have someone to answer to for letting this fear choke the life out of the gift you have been given."

Linda knew that he was right. She recalled her talks with Dorian about the very same thing. But now she was mad. He did not know her situation. What right did he have to judge her?

She got up in his face and said, yelling, "You know, your speech reminds of one of those bad made for television, the Church is the way, movies."

"I didn't say anything about the Church," Julian interjected. But Linda did not skip a beat.

"You seem to know so much. You seem to have all of the answers. You seem to know exactly what I am going through. Come on now; say something that will really strike me. Come on Mr. Noel. I hope you are not trying to save me with this weak, tired, useless rhetoric."

Julian looked into the eyes of the wounded creature before him. He knew that he was pushing a little too hard. He changed the mood giving her a little sly smile and then asked her, "Will you accompany me to the symposium ball tonight?"

Linda in a total state of shock could only respond with a tone, "Huh?"

"Will you go to the dance with me tonight?"

Linda stood there and just stared at him. The emotional roller coaster that Julian was taking her on was so overwhelming but in a good way. Even though he was infuriating her, he was touching places within her soul that had never been touched before. It wasn't because he was the most beautiful man that she had ever seen, even though he was. It was something about his inner strength that reached way deep inside of her, healing the hurt and she could not figure out how.

Julian waiting for her to answer said, "Come on now Linda that was not a rhetorical question."

Linda not knowing what to say answered, "I don't have anything to wear."

"That is an excuse, not an answer. Still avoiding."

"It's not an excuse. It is the truth."

Julian walked down the beach a little more. "Ok. If that problem is taken care of, will you go to the dance with me?"

Linda felt the blood rushing to her face. It had been so long since she had been out with a man. Not that she was thinking that this was a date but it was a date. She could not conceal her smile. She answered. "Well, yes I guess."

"Great," Julian responded. "Meet me in the lobby, after you are finished with this afternoon's meet and greet."

Linda's smile disappeared from her face. "Who said I was going to that?"

"Why wouldn't you? You started well last night. Why let the momentum die. A publishing deal is not going to just drop in your lap."

"Who said that I was looking for a deal?" Linda asked becoming defensive again.

Julian pretended to show signs of becoming frustrated with her. "Did you not just tell me that your son is the most important thing to you? Do you think that seeing you operate below your ability is a good example for him?

Linda does not answer for a moment. Once again she knew Julian was right. She just did not want him to know that she knew. She bent down and picked up a handful of sand and threw it at him. "You know what? You are getting on my nerves."

Julian dusts the sand off of his shirt and walked up the beach. "Good." He said. "Wouldn't have it any other way." He continued walking away from Linda. "You have a meet and greet to go to. See you later."

Linda turned away from Julian for a moment so that he could not see her talking to herself. "He's got a lot of nerve." Linda looked out over the ocean for one more moment and then turned back around to talk to Julian. To her surprise however Julian was nowhere to be found. "Julian." She called out. Linda walked in the direction that had Julian walked. She could not even find his footprints in the sand. She thought that the water waves washed them away. "Julian." She called out again. "Where did he go?" She stopped for a moment and pulled the paper out of her pocket that she had taken from him.

A diamond you are but your glimmer you hide.

Fear is the cloak. Your freedom it chides. 'How

dare you want to be free it says. It's your own

fault that I am here. To get rid of me, you can't' –

That's the power of fear.

But look up and look out into the face of Love's

True glory. Look hard Linda and then you will see,

P.S. from above, it's not the end of your story.

She folded the paper and put it back into her pocket. She walked over to the water. She removed her clothes, revealing undergarments that look like swimwear. She stepped into the churning waves, going forward until the water is well above her waist. She took a deep breath and closed her eyes. She spread out her arms to her side and began to float on her back.

"Lord, I'm looking into the face of loves true glory. Help me, please. Help my son." A tender sweet presence came over her. And for the first time in a long time, Linda was at rest floating effortlessly upon the water.

In the distance, Carlos stood on some rocks. He was looking at Linda through a pair of binoculars. He lowered them and watched her wade in the water. He reached into his pocket and pulled out a diamond wedding ring. He looked intently at it for a moment and then flung it out into the ocean.

"Soon." He said and walked away.

21

Cameron and Salomé arrived back at the hotel. There was now a sea of people - 100 times as many that had been there in the morning. "Now how are we going to find her? Look at all of these people. She could be anywhere." Cameron said.

Salomé parked the car. The wheels were turning in her head. They had to find her. "Page, we'll have her paged." She suggested to Cameron. They jumped out of the car and ran towards the entrance. Linda was walking up at the same time. Her hair was wet and windblown from being on the beach and in the water. Her encounter on the beach had given her the strength to go to the meet and greet. Julian was right. It could not hurt a thing. As Linda was about to go inside, Salomé and Cameron came running up and pushed Linda aside.

Cameron said as he pushed Linda, "Out of the way coming through Ms. Please excuse us." As they burst through the door, they realized that they had just run over the very person they were looking for. They stopped and looked at each other. Salomé hit Cameron in the arm. "See what you did."

"What I did?" Cameron bit back. They ran back outside as Linda was composing herself.

109

"Oh my God, Ms. Andrews we are so sorry," Salomé said with remorse.

Linda had recovered for her near tumble. "That's ok. Boy, you two are sure in a hurry."

"Yes, to find you," Salomé said.

"Excuse me?" Linda replied.

"I have wanted to talk to you since last night. I don't know if you recall but I told you that I am a JR. Editor for Giles Publishing. This is my associate Mr. Cameron Day."

"Please to meet you again." He shook Linda's hand.

People were continually flowing through the front entrance. It began to crowd them out as well as getting louder.

Salomé, knowing that they needed to get to a less busy place asked Linda if they could go back to her suite. Linda peeped over at Cameron with an uneasy gaze. He recognized it and said, "Excuse me ladies but Salomé I need to go and take care of that matter we discussed earlier." Salomé, not understanding what he was doing looked at him confused. Cameron continued. "So I will not be able to accompany you and Ms. Andrews to your suite."

"Oh, ok that's fine." She answered him, finally understanding what he was doing. "Ms. Andrews, it looks like it will be just you and me."

Linda agreed. "Ok. I'll talk to you. But for the life of me, I don't understand why."

"Well let's go talk and I will tell you why," Salomé stated.

Julian walked in and talked to the sales lady in the boutique. It was a full-service boutique. One could find everything from Clothes, Shoes, Hair, and Make-up. Julian pointed to some specific items. He shook the hand of the sales lady and departed. He walked into the hotel's business center and sat down at a computer. He typed some information in and then pulled his notebook out of his pocket. He once again writes some notes under a name already printed in the notebook – Dorian Andrews.

22

The phone rang while Mrs. Winder was in the kitchen of Linda's house, getting Dorian's snack ready. She pranced over to answer the phone. "Hello. Yes, it is." She said responding to the question. "This is who? Oh my, how exciting. Yes, go ahead." She reached for a piece of paper to write down the information that she was receiving from the person on the phone.

Linda and Salomé reached the hotel suite. "Come on in and have a seat," Salomé said to Linda. Linda walked into the room but did not seem to be impressed with being surrounded by the expensive beautiful furnishings. Most people who lived in a place like Linda's would have been awestruck.

"Do you want anything to drink?" Salomé asked.

"Sure, some juice please," Linda responded. She spotted a Faberge vase sitting on the table in the room. She picked it up and studied it. "Tiffany. This hotel spares no expense." Salomé returned with a glass of wine in her hand and juice for Linda. She handed it to her and took a sip of her wine. She examined the vase in Linda's hands herself.

"Yes, you are exactly right. Do you work with fine furnishings?"

Linda put the vase back on the table, took the glass of juice that was being extended to her, took a sip and answered, "No, I'm a waitress." She took another sip of her juice and sat down.

Salomé tried not to look shocked. She thought to herself, "How could a waitress know of such things?" She then began to feel guilty for her egregious attitude but could not help but to say to Linda, "I hope that this statement does not offend you, but your demeanor does not reflect that of a waitress. You seem to be much more refined than that."

"Well, I guess being refined is relative. I have always found that culture or refinement is a state of being and attitude not a vocation." Linda answered.

"I don't mean to offend you."

Linda said, "You didn't. But I tell you what – I'll just go ahead and give you my stats. That way I will let you off the hook of trying to find the right words to say." Salomé just nodded her head. She did not want to aggravate the situation anymore.

Linda continued. "I entered college at the age of 16. I earned a degree in English from Bennington University. I was getting ready to start working on my Master's when I got pregnant. So I stopped. I am not married but I have a son, 10, who is now in a private school for the musically gifted."

"Wow," Salomé said. "A private school. Does your job cover that or does he receive a scholarship?"

"He has a partial one. The rest comes out of my pocket."

"Must be rough."

"I cut corners on the frivolous things. Our home is not the grandest but it is clean and in a safe neighborhood."

Salomé asked, "With an English degree, couldn't you have gotten a better job?" Linda did not answer her question. Salomé continued along with the same topic. "Normally, as a professional woman, I would throw my two cents in and say, why don't you go back to school and get your Masters? But you would say…"

"I could not do that and pay for my baby's schooling."

Salomé said, "Then I would answer with, what I called you up here to discuss will solve that problem."

"How so?" Linda asked.

"Now I'm going to get right to the point. I want to offer you a contract with Giles Publishing."

"A contract to do what?"

"Well let me think, to bus the employee cafeteria, to write of course," Salomé answered Linda.

"To write what?"

Salomé could not believe her ears. "Ok, now you are scaring me."

Linda put her glass down on the table. "The only thing that you read of mine was an impromptu poem and now you want to offer me a writing contract?"

"Yes," Salomé said emphatically.

"Why on earth? I can't conceive this." Said Linda.

"Look." Salomé projected as she sat up more erected. She wanted Linda to know how serious she was. "You have something special. It's the simplicity in which you write. It's your passion. It's how shut off you are but an essence still exudes from you that cannot be denied. Yes, I only saw one poem but in those few words, I recognized a writer that has something this world desperately needs."

Linda got up out of her seat and paced around the room. Why was everyone trying to tell her about what she had to offer? "Boy is that the business company line? 'You have something that this world needs'?"

Salomé tried to defuse the situation that she feared was getting out of control. "I'm sorry if…"

Linda cut her off. "Look, right now my life is not about me. The chapters were written and the book was closed on me years ago. Now it's all about my son."

Salomé could no longer hold back her emotions. She stood up as well. "Ok, I grant you that. It is all about your son. Well, would $100,000.00 help you with his story?"

Linda whirled around and faced Salomé. "My son needs more than money."

"Yes, but I am sure that his school is not going to look after that or even care about that. $100,000.00 is just to start. With your talent…"

Linda broke in on her again. "I'm sorry. Who offers an unknown author a contract like that? $1000 maybe but $100,000, give me a break. Plus, I just can't see all of this talent that you see."

"Is it that you don't see it or are you afraid for it to be seen by others?" Salomé asked. Linda does not answer her question. Salomé sensed that there was more going on with Linda than she was letting on. She did not know her but she knew that somehow she must help her.

Linda was determined to keep her low profile. She could not afford to be put into the spotlight. "Ms. Davenport, you are talking about a major deal that would include a lot of PR work correct?" "Yes, that is the standard," Salomé answered.

"Then how do you expect me to travel all over the country while I have a young son in school?"

"Promotional tours don't last all year," Salomé told her in an attempt to comfort her. "Perhaps he could stay with relatives."

Linda snapped. "There are no other relatives."

 "Maybe the boy's father could..." Salomé could not believe that those words had come out of her mouth. But it was too late now. However, Linda took it, if necessary, Salomé would try to provide damage control.

Linda glared at Salomé. Only dead silence filled the room. There was nothing to break the eerie quiet, not even the sound of their breath. Only maybe the slight sloshing coming from Salomé's wine glass as her hands began to tremble. Neither one of them spoke for what seemed like an eternity. Finally, Linda calmly said, "As I recall, I told you that I was not married. It is just me and my son Dorian." She tossed her head back. "Why am I explaining myself again?" She addressed Salomé.

"I need to go." Linda headed toward the door. But she had a strange desire for Salomé to reach out to her and stop her. She could not understand herself. Her fear made her want to leave, but something else within her was crying out for Salomé to help her stay. Her silent cry for help must have been heard because Salomé flung herself in front of the door, not allowing Linda to leave.

"Linda wait, please. I'm sorry. I know I came on strong. But I see something in you. We can work it out. My boss is coming here to meet you. I know that we can work something out. Please, just give it and yourself a chance. You have managed to do great things for your son already with limited resources. You have made great sacrifices for him. Don't give up on him now or yourself because you can't see how you would do it."

Salomé saw in Linda's eyes a sign of surrender. Linda leaned against the wall and slid down to the ground. Salomé did the same. For whatever reason Salomé told Linda one more thing that she felt Linda needed to hear and which she meant from her heart.

"You won't be alone. Not this time."

Linda dropped her head trying to conceal the tears in her eyes. "Ms. Davenport?"

"Salomé Please."

"Salomé, do I really…" She hesitated with the rest of her question. A few of Julian's words ran through her mind, 'It's not the end of your story.' She straightened her back and with a more confident tone continued. "You think that I can do it? You think that I am good enough – because I can't fail. I can't fail my son."

Salomé began to reflect upon her own experiences within the past couple of days and repeated some of the wisdom that Mr. Giles had given to her. "Do you want to know the truth? It's not what I think, feel or believe that matters. What matters is what you think. Let me share something with you. Before I came here, I was coming off of some terrible reviews concerning two authors that I signed to the company."

Linda teased, "Oh now that is building my confidence."

Salomé came back with, "Oh so you have jokes. Anyway – I was feeling pretty low about my abilities and myself. Criticism can be a hard pill to swallow. Criticism with malice can be downright crippling and in this business, it is always with malice. Anyway, my boss called me into his office right after these reviews came out. Do you know why?"

Linda looked at Salomé wondering how she was expected to answer. "Not really."

Salomé answered. "He called me in, to send me here to find the companies next top writer. He told me 'Hodge Pudgy,' whatever that means, to what the critics say and just go with my God-given talents and instincts. The critics may have not loved my choices but the people have. And my instincts tell me that the people will love you too."

Linda sat there meditating on what Salomé had just said. For the first time in a long time, she began to let her defenses down. "You know, I have had some critics in my life as well."

"I can tell," Salomé responded.

"How Salomé? How do you get over and beyond the crippling effects? I have so many demons that haunt me. How do I defeat that which is stronger than I am?"

Salomé was a little unnerved by the question but tried to answer from her heart. "For me, I just remember that there is one who is stronger than all the demons and bigger than all of my fears. He is always there with us to protect and deliver us. Even when we can't seem to feel Him or see His love in the midst of ugliness – He is always there."

Linda just sat silently for a while. Salomé was praying that she had not sermonized her. She just spoke from her heart. Finally, Linda spoke up. "May I have a sip of that?" pointing to the wine glass. Salomé hands it to her. She takes a sip and says, "I'll meet with your boss. And we can discuss the details of the contract."

Salomé's eyes widened, as she was not able to contain her excitement. "Are you – are you for real? Yes?"

"Yes," Linda answered with a big smile on her face. But one thing, this is the weakest wine I have ever tasted before in my life." She hands the glass back.

"That's because it's non-alcoholic."

Salomé and Linda get up laughing and hug. After they released Salomé remembered a request from Mr. Giles. "Oh, Mr. Giles is going to want to look at some more of your work."

"Can't you show him the poem from last night?"

"I did that," Salomé said. "That's why he wants to see more. You do have some other writings?"

Linda responded. "Oh girl, shoot yes. I have plenty." Linda was lying because she didn't know what to say. She had lots of things written in journals but nothing that she thought would be good enough to publish. She started for the door again.

Salomé walked with her and said, "Great Mr. Giles will be here tomorrow."

"Can't wait," Linda said trying to convince herself. They hug one more time and Linda left heading towards the elevator. As Salomé was watching her the phone rang.

"Hello."

It was Cameron on the other end. "Hey, I'm sorry but how is it going?"

"You mean congratulations don't you?" Salomé said smiling.

"You mean she has agreed to sign?" Cameron asked.

"That is exactly what I mean." Salomé whirled and twirled around the room.

23

Linda came bolting off of the elevator and crashed into Julian. She hurried to get up off the ground and started heading for the exit. Julian got up and ran after her. "Linda, what the…"

Linda seemed to have been inoculated with the speed of Flo Jo. "Linda, woman, will you stop!" Julian yelled after her.

"I can't. I got to go." She yelled back to him out of breath.

Julian finally caught up to her and stopped her. "Oh no, we have a deal."

Linda answered him frantically. She spoke so fast that she hardly took a breath. "No, you don't understand. Mr. Giles is coming here to see me. He wants to read some of my other writings. I don't have any other writings - At least not good ones. They offered me $100,000.00. Not that money is everything but it can do so much. I don't have anything prepared."

Julian cut in. "Stop. Slow down. You are only supposed to get ready for the dance. That's all."

Linda remembered that she had said yes to Julian's invitation. How could she possibly go now? She had to go home

and write. "Oh my God, the dance. I can't go. I don't have time."
She tried to run but Julian won't let her.

"Oh no. You promised and I got everything set up."

Linda was beside herself. "Haven't you been listening to
me? I have to go write!

"Why?" Julian asked as if he had no idea what was going
on.

Linda rolled her eyes at him. "You are getting on my
nerves again. As I said, I have been offered a contract and they
want to see some more of my writings. I don't have anything to
show them. So I have to go home and write. You goober."

"Say that again."

"You goober," Linda repeated.

Julian glared at Linda. "No, smarty, the other thing."

"What, that I have been offered a contract?" It dawned on
Linda what she was saying. "I have been offered a writing
contract."

She jumped up and down and jumped into Julian's arms.
For a moment, time seemed to have stopped for Linda. Julian's
arms were so strong. He held her up in the air and spun her

around. They laughed and celebrated. Then as he put her back down, he just held her for a moment. Linda felt so free - so alive. There was nothing erotic in the way he held her. She just felt love and support. She had never experienced that from a man before.

After a moment Linda came back to reality. "Julian about the dance, I can't make it. I have to go and write."

"You can't afford to miss this trust me," Julian said to her.

"But Julian…" She tried to protest.

"Just relax," Julian told her as he massaged her shoulders. "I will help you prepare something but you need to be at the dance tonight."

Linda shook her head with doubt. "I don't know."

"Will you please stop trying to control everything in your life? Now come on." Julian took her by the hand and led her to the boutique. On the outside of the door, there is a sign indicating that it was closed for the afternoon. Julian knocked on the door. A man dressed in a Tuxedo opened the doors.

"Ms. Andrews. Welcome. We have been waiting for you. Please come in." The boutique was decorated with all types of exotic flowers and there were all kinds of foods laid out on a table.

There were also people there who would pamper Linda from head to toe.

"Is all of this for me?" Linda asked in total surprise.

"Yes, ma'am. Whatever you need, it's here."

Linda looked around amazed. "Well, color me the pretty woman."

She received a massage, soaked in a tub, and received a manicure and a pedicure. As her hair was being done, she was presented with all types of evening gowns and shoes. She was having the time of her life.

Julian smiled as he watched a woman who was once dead come alive again. He knew that it had nothing to do with the material things that she was receiving. It just had to do with her being treated with mercy and kindness. Someone was showing her the truth – she mattered. He walked over to her to let her know that he was leaving to get ready himself. She just smiled at him. Julian smiled back and left.

24

The lobby was filled with the men in black tie and women in beautiful evening gowns. Julian was in his tux with a white jacket and black pants. He walked back towards the boutique to pick up Linda. Mr. Keller stopped him for a moment.

"Well good evening to you Mr. Noel. Are you ready to enjoy the evening's festivities?"

"Yes sir, I am," Julian responded. Julian could tell from Mr. Keller's demeanor that he was not there just to exchange simple pleasantries. His deduction was quickly confirmed.

"I've been informed that a pretty big tab has been accumulated in our boutique."

"Um, hmm," Julian mumbled as he continued to look around at all of the people.

Mr. Keller put his hands behind his back, dropped his head for a moment and then looked back up at Julian with a grin on his face. "You remember when I told you that everything would be on the house for you during your stay here."

"Oh yes sir I do and I appreciate it." Julian turned away from Mr. Keller who was showing signs of stress over the situation.

"You do understand that I meant everything for you, would be on the house." His British accent became thick and heavy.

 "Oh yes of course," Julian answered. He decided to let Mr. Keller of the hook. But Mr. Keller insisted on making sure that he was understood.

"I mean no disrespect; I just wanted to make sure that there were no miss understandings. You know how merchants can be."

"Of course and no miss understandings. None what so ever." Julian replied quickly wanting to wrap up the conversation. "Well, I have to go pick up my date."

Mr. Keller clicked his heels and extended his hand towards Julian. "Certainly." They shook hands and Julian walked away. Mr. Keller walked over to a house phone and dialed a number.

"Front desk. This is Mr. Keller. Make sure that Mr. Noel's little My Fair Lady experiment gets charged to his room." He hung up the phone and continued to greet partygoers.

Julian arrived at the boutique but found the doors closed. He knocked on the door but there is no answer. He knocked again.

He heard the sound of the lock in the tumblers. Julian stepped back as the doors began to open. The workers were standing there in parallel lines. From around the corner, Linda emerged.

Julian could not believe his eyes as he watched the ninth wonder of the world walk towards him. The only words that he could muster were, "Oh my goodness." Linda was an angelic vision. The royal blue colored evening gown, full and flowing made her look like a princess. She possessed a majestic beauty that had been hidden and wounded. The years of pain had melted away and life and vitality defined her swagger now.

"My Mr. Noel - You clean up well."

"And you look like I knew you would. You are absolutely beautiful."

Linda felt on top of the world. The look in Julian's eyes made her feel whole and complete. "You know what they say, 'flattery will get you almost everywhere'." She said to Julian.

"I thought that the saying was, 'flattery will get you everywhere'." He responded as he extended his arm.

Linda took his arm and playfully replied, "I'm a writer Julian. Have you never heard of Poetic License?" They both laughed and they walked toward the ballroom.

25

The music coming from the dance hall was intoxicating. Linda let her eyes close slightly allowing the melodies to envelop her. As they arrived at the doors, they swung open in unison to reveal a room full of dancers floating across the floor in a rhythmic motion. All the men were dressed in black tuxedos and the women in colorful evening gowns. The dancers all donned masks fashioned in the form of leaves - multihued with the colors of fall. As they spun and dipped and twirled, it appeared as if the mask where leaves floating through the air as they fell from mystical trees.

Linda and Julian received their masks. Linda gathered herself as the atmosphere was absorbing her. She stopped before she put on her mask and said to Julian, "Now you know that I can't stay long. I have some writing to do."

"Will you just relax?" Julian said to her smiling. "This is your night just enjoy it."

From across the room, Cameron and Salomé were eating some hors d' oeuvres. Cameron spotted Linda and was captivated by this closed-off waitress turned into a strong, confident, beautiful woman.

"Man, will you look at that," Cameron said with his eyes fixated on Linda.

"What?" Salomé asked as she turned to see what Cameron was looking at. "Wow!" She said as she noticed that Cameron was still staring. "Hey, stop looking so hard." She elbowed him in the stomach, which caused Cameron to spew out a sushi roll that he had just put in his mouth.

"Come on baby, you know that you are the only one for me." Salome' smiled and picked up his dislodged mishap with a napkin.

Just before Linda and Julian put on their mask, Linda leaned over and kissed him on the cheek. "Thank you for giving me the best time I've had in a long time."

Julian caressed her face. "It's not me. It's you allowing yourself to enjoy it. May I have this dance?"

"You most certainly may." They walked onto the dance floor and joined in with the ballroom ballet. Mixed into the crowd, a lone man was wearing a red tuxedo jacket. His mask covered his whole face and he was not interested in the dance at all. He was only interested in Linda.

The man watched Linda dance with Julian. As Julian and Linda danced and turned, the man moved closer and closer to them. In an instant, as Julian twirled Linda where she faced a couple dancing behind them, the same couple spun away from Julian and Linda putting the stranger right there behind Julian's back. Linda pulled up and gasps at the sight of this man in his full mask and red jacket. She could sense that this man was staring right through her. Julian turned by reflex to see what had startled Linda. By this time another couple had danced in behind them. When they twirled, the masked man was nowhere to be found.

"Linda, are you ok?" Julian asked as he watched his dance partner.

"There was a man…" She stopped speaking looking around trying to find the stranger.

Julian walked off the dance floor with Linda and pulled her to the side. "Linda, there are tons of men here."

"No, this man had on a full mask and a red tuxedo jacket. He just stared at me. Like he knew me." Julian continued to look around but all he could see were men in black jackets.

"I don't see anyone dressed like that. Come on, let's finish our dance." Linda looked around the room. The incident gave her chills. It was the red jacket. That was the favorite color of the foe from her past. Plus the man's gaze - it had the look of death. Julian was right though; no one was in the hall anymore dressed like that.

She relaxed and decided that she would not let the demons from her past interfere with the fun she was having tonight.

The masked ballet came to an end. The dancing continued, however. Linda and Julian were getting a lot of attention. It could not be otherwise. They looked like royalty out on the floor. People, who remembered Linda from the poetry reading/clinic from the night before, came up to talk with her. Julian stayed in the background as much as he could. He knew that this would be a night that Linda would never forget.

Salomé and Cameron were finished eating and decided that they were going to get their Tic Tok worthy dance on. As they turned to walk to the dance floor, they were wrought with surprise as they bump into Mr. Giles.

Salomé was shocked. "Mr. Giles, what are you doing here? You weren't supposed to be here until tomorrow."

The distinguished Mr. Giles was shadow dancing to the music. He answered. "Now you didn't think that I was going to let you have all the fun, did you?

"No sir, I guess not," Salomé answered.

"Oh, by the way, is that clever writer that you discovered here tonight?"

"She sure is. Right over there." Salomé pointed out Linda to Mr. Giles.

He looked over in the direction of Linda and the glowing aura of his new author enthralled him. "Clever and extremely stunning. Is that her husband?"

"No. She's not married. That's Julian Noel, a world-renowned author." Salomé told him.

Mr. Giles responded with a quizzical look on his face. "Hmm. Never heard of him."

"Me either," Cameron interjected as he put his arm around Simon's shoulder. Mr. Giles stared at him. Cameron removed his arm from around Mr. Giles and giggled. To Cameron's good fortune, a beautiful woman in her late 50's ambled up to Simon. It was his wife.

"Good evening everyone." She greeted the employees of her husband with grace and elegance. "Simon, are you going to let your wife become a wallflower?"

"Of course not dear." He took her hand and turned to Salomé, "When you can arrange it, I would like to go ahead and meet Ms. Andrews tonight."

"Yes, sir," Salomé answered in the affirmative.

"Have fun you two." He danced onto the floor with his wife in tow. Salomé and Cameron walked over to Linda and Julian. They had stepped off the dance floor and were partaking of the delectable foods provided for the partygoers. They were still talking to the constant parade of well-wishers.

"Hi, Linda. Girl, you are looking fierce." Salomé complimented her.

"Oh stop Salomé," Linda replied trying to give the appearance of humility even though she loved all of the attention she was receiving.

She turned to Cameron and addressed him. "Hi, Cameron right?"

"Yeah, that's right." Cameron smiled.

Linda turned into the direction of Julian. "I'm sure that you know Mr. Julian Noel."

"Remember him but…" Cameron replied but was not able to complete his sentence because Salomé interrupted him.

"We sure do." They shook hands with him. Cameron still looked at him crossways.

Salomé continued. "Linda, Mr. Giles is here at the Ball tonight and wants to meet you."

"He's what? I thought he wasn't supposed to be here until tomorrow." Linda said with panic in her voice.

"He came in for the Ball."

Linda looked over at Julian. He just smiled at her. She took a deep breath and full of resolve asked Salomé, "Where is he? I can't wait to meet him?"

Salomé was taken aback by the quickness of Linda's response. She looked around for Mr. Giles. "Well, ok. There he is."

Linda said to Julian, "I have some business to take care of. I will be right back."

As she is walked away with Salomé, Julian called out to her, "Hey..." Linda looks back. "I like the way that you are coming out of your comfort zone." Linda winked at him and goes over to meet Mr. Giles.

"What a Lotus blossom," Cameron said.

"Like I said before. All it takes is a little patience." Julian replied and then walked away.

"When did you say that?" Cameron asked but he did not notice that Julian had walked away. Cameron looked around but could not locate him. "Man, who is this guy?"

26

Linda shook Mr. Giles's hand and said good night to him and his wife. She went back to find Julian but she did not see him. "Where did he go?" She thought to herself. "I was only gone for a moment. Men."

She continued looking for him as the Master of Ceremony, who was dressed in a black tux with tales and a top hat, took the stage. "Ladies and gentlemen, may I have our attention please." Linda was still scanning the room when the lights went down and a spotlight highlighted the Master of Ceremony on the stage. "Is everyone having a good time?" He waited for the claps and the whistles of the crowd to die down before he continued. Linda had given up her effort to find Julian. It was much too dark in the room now. The MC continued. "We have come to the part of our event where we would like to thank our many sponsors who help to make this symposium possible."

The hall filled with a thunderous round of applause from a grateful crowd. They were thanking the many philanthropic donors who helped to make their dreams come true. The MC continued. "For some of you who may not know, these same sponsors also provide money for scholarships, paid through the symposiums foundation, to people right here in our very own community in all areas of the arts, writing, drama, painting, and music."

At hearing this Linda perked up and listened more. She was thinking that she may be able to get help for Dorian.

"Community is very important to us - especially the children in our community. Every 5 years we showcase a child, which displays exceptional talent in the area of the arts. This year, thanks to being tipped off by Mr. Julian Noel, we present to you, a 10-year-old virtuoso of music. Ladies and Gentlemen, I present to you, Maestro Dorian Andrews."

Linda raised her hands to her face and tears ran down her cheeks as she watched her son take the stage in a sharp tux of his own. He waved and smiled at Linda, then sat down and began to play Linda's favorite classical song. As the crowd was mesmerized by Dorian's playing, Julian walked up behind Linda.

She turned and gazed at him in disbelief. He had brought a miracle into her life. A life that she felt was dead and in the grave. They did not speak. No words needed to be said. He wiped the tears from her face. He took her in his arms and they hugged. Unspoken words of love exchanged between them. A love that goes deeper than the physical. Linda was experiencing for the first time in her life an agape love. Love that was given to her with no strings attached.

Dorian finished playing and bowed towards a crowd that was going wild - Linda most of all. The MC came back on stage and addressed the crowd. "Oh my - the talent that we have here tonight. Hi, there young man."

"Hi," Dorian said back with a smile as big as the moon on his face. He definitely didn't assimilate his mother's shy bug.

"You are incredible, do you know that?" The MC directed his question toward Dorian.

"Well sir, it is the gift giver that's incredible," Dorian said to him. The crowd clapped and Julian loudest of all at this statement from one so young.

The MC said, "I want everyone to know that this has not been just another symposium, oh no. This young man happens to be the son of the fine young writer that we were introduced to last night, Ms. Linda Andrews. Ms. Andrews can you come up here please." Julian escorted her to the stage. He remembered how just the night before he was trying to stop her from running out of the place.

Linda took the stage and Dorian ran over to her and gave her a big hug.

"Say, mom. You look hot." Dorian said shaking his head up and down with his hands in his pocket as he stood back to admire her. The crowd lets out a laugh as their hearts are filled with warmth as they watch the mother and son exchange pleasantries that indicate a true closeness and pureness of affection. The MC went on to tell the crowd of the forthcoming writing contract that Linda would be signing with Giles Publishing.

Dorian jumped up and down and shouted, "I told you. I told you that you could do it, mom." From the back of the crowd, Simon Giles informed them that there was one more surprise.

He took the stage and without even asking, the MC handed him the microphone. "It has been brought to my attention that you are worried about the continuation of your son's music training with the possibility of a heavy promotion schedule. Well, worry no more. After seeing what I have seen here tonight, I have decided to add a monetary allowance to your contract that will cover the cost of a private music tutor for your son. So when you travel, he can travel with you."

Linda stood there in astonishment. Dorian ran over to the piano and began to play his favorite boogie-woogie song.

Julian stepped up behind Salomé and whispered in her ear, "See what can happen when you forget about your critics – your problems and follow your instincts, your God-given talents, and your heart." Salomé turned around but saw one there.

The MC was bringing everything back to order again. It was a hard feat for him to accomplish. This was the most exciting symposium Havocy Bay had ever experienced.

"Well, I would like to thank everyone for showing up tonight. We just have one more thing to do this evening. Master Dorian, will you please choose the final dance for tonight."

Dorian walked around the stage for the moment. He put his hands behind his back, dropped his head thinking - as if he was trying to find the answer to the meaning of life. Finally, he said, "Let's go Bollywood!"

"Well, you heard him, ladies and gents. Band, hit it." The band began to play and everyone started to dance. Julian and Dorian along with Linda joined in. Salomé and Cameron stood in shock as they saw Ravi leading the way.

From the back of the room, Carlos Andres stood and watched the happy trio. No one noticed him sharpening a little mini knife on a sharpening block. He took the knife and flung it across the room. It struck a pillar that had been decorated with balloons, that was close to Linda and Julian. The knife caused some of the balloons to explode. It frightened Linda even though the sound was slightly muffled by the band playing. She looked up along with Julian as they kept dancing.

"Just some balloons," Julian told her. They could not see the small knife that had been embedded in the pillar. As they continued to dance, Julian's attention was drawn to the back of the room. He saw a man exiting the room wearing a red jacket.

"What are you looking at?" Linda asked him.

"Nothing. Nothing at all." Julian remembered that earlier Linda had mentioned an out of place man in a red tux jacket that had unnerved her. He excused himself for a moment. He stepped to the side as the assembly was still dancing. Dorian and Linda were still having the time of their lives. Julian pulled his notebook out of his pocket and opened it up. Inside was a name printed in red, Carlos Andres. Julian's eyes widened as he looked at the name.

The band had finally stopped playing and everyone was beginning to exit. Julian closed the notebook and rushed back over to Linda and Dorian. They were talking to Salomé, Cameron, Mr. Giles, and his wife. Julian was not interested in their conversation. He was only concerned with the pillar that the balloons exploded on. Discreetly he studied the pillar. He found what he was looking for. He saw the knife.

27

Julian and Dorian were in Linda's living room playing the thumb war game. "One, two, three, four, I declare a thumb war…" Julian and Dorian were chanting in unison. Linda was in the kitchen fixing coffee. They had all changed back into regular clothes. Linda was in a top and only pair of nice Jeans. It did not bother her though. She would be able to pick up a few things now that she had a new gig. Not that material things were important to her. In her eyes, things were a necessity - not what defined her.

She filled the two mixed matched coffee cups with water and two scoops of instant coffee. She placed the cups into the microwave and pushed the start button. While she was waiting for it to finish she listened to her son laugh and play with Julian. She was thankful for that. She understood how important a man's influence in her son's life would be. Not that she was thinking that it would be Julian. She could tell from the way he was in the café that putting down roots was not something in his plans at the moment.

The microwave beeped. She removed the coffee cups with steam rising. She breathed in deeply the aroma of the instant coffee and called out to Julian, "Julian, what do you take in your coffee?"

"Tons of cream and sugar." He answered.

"I'll just have mine black mom," Dorian yelled back. Linda came into the living room from the kitchen with only two cups of coffee and one glass of chocolate milk in her hand.

Julian was impressed that she could carry it all but remembered that she was a waitress. He took the cup that Linda directed at him. "Black you say." Linda looked at Dorian with a little smirk on her face and handed him his glass of milk. "This is the darkest beverage that you will get tonight."

Dorian took the glass and gulped it down. He wiped his mouth on his sleeve. "Aha, delicious." Linda was about to correct him for wiping his mouth on his sleeve but decided to leave it alone for the night.

"Alright, little man, Mr. Noel and I have to get some work done. Why don't you go to your room and read."

Dorian let out a sigh and shook his finger at his mom. "Only because I know you have work to do."

"Excuse me, mister?" Linda looked fiercely at Dorian.

"What?" Dorian said innocently. "I just said that I need to go to my room so you can get some work done." He smiled at

Linda and walked away. He stopped and walked back to Julian. "Mr. Noel?"

"Yes, Dorian." Julian bent down to become eye level with Dorian.

"Thank you for doing what you did tonight. And thank you for being so nice to my mom." He extended his hand to Julian. Julian took it but then Dorian hugged him. Julian reciprocated after which Dorian departed for his room. But not before he went over and got a kiss from his mom.

"See you later sweetie," Linda said as she watched her true miracle walk to his room.

"That is a great kid," Julian said. "I see why you said that you would do anything for him."

" Yes, he's worth it," Linda said.

"Do you know that you are worth it?" Julian asked.

Linda felt herself beginning to blush so she changed the subject. "Ok dude, can we just get to writing?"

"Yes, I guess you had better." Julian stood up and started looking around the room. He spotted a well-read bible on the shelf and a crucifix on the wall.

Linda questioned, "What do you mean I? Don't you mean we?"

"I don't have a publishing contract. You do." He picked up a ball that was sitting on the shelf and began to toss it up in the air and catching it.

"But you said that you would help." Linda protested.

"Yes help, not write. You have to do that yourself."

Linda was not believing her eyes or hearing her ears. Gone was her Prince charming. The same standoffish customer had replaced him that she first encountered in the café. "Write! Write! Write what?" Linda said infuriated.

Julian rolled his eyes at her. "Why do you make this so difficult? It is in you girl. Just let it out."

"Let what out?"

"Haven't you learned anything this evening? The love girl. That is the only thing that will make a difference."

Linda dropped her head. "I don't know how to let it out."

"I know," Julian said to her. "You keep looking at yourself and your so-called limitations – your mistakes. You can't write with that kind of negative energy. People don't want what they already have. They want to know that the impossible is possible."

Linda looked at him confused. "What… are you… talking about?"

"People have plenty to show them what is wrong and bad in their lives. You are here to show them what is right and good. You are here to return to them the hope, that the world and the evils of it, have stripped them of. Your job is to remind them of the truth and the only way to do that is to…" Julian stopped talking to let Linda think of the answer. He knew that she knew it. She would have to realize that fact herself.

Linda pondered. She looked over at the cross hanging on the wall and said, "The only way to remind them is to have them look into the face of Love's true Glory."

"There you go," Julian said excitedly. "But there is another aspect that goes with looking into this face."

"What is that?" Linda asked.

"Forgiving." He answered.

"Forgiving? What? Who?" Linda questioned.

Julian turned and looked deeply into her eyes. He wanted to make sure that she fully understood the point that he was about to make. "Anybody who has hurt you. Even yourself."

"Myself? Forgiving ourselves? Is that important or even necessary?" Linda asked her question with intense determination to understand what he meant.

"Oh yes. Not forgiving ourselves is often the most overlooked principle in our lives. Not that I prescribe to principles or formulas for living. But un-forgiveness is a cancer that eats away at the very core of our being. Destroying our lives.

Linda turned away from Julian so that he could not look into her eyes. She was afraid that he would be able to tell that she was hiding something. "But what if what you have done or what someone else has done to you is just too horrible to forgive?"

"That's easy to answer. There does not exist anything in this world that cannot be forgiven."

Linda was taken aback by his answer. "You believe that don't you?"

Julian walked over to the shelf and took the Bible off of it. "I really know that. You would know it too if you opened your heart to truly believed what you read in here – reading it is not enough" he said as he waved the Bible up in the air. Linda gawked at him in a panic. She did not want him to open it up. She walked over to him and took the Bible from him and returned it to the shelf.

"What makes you think that I don't believe what's in here?"

"Our conversation maybe."

Linda continued. "So you believe that God will forgive everything?"

"Yep."

"No matter what?" Linda asked.

"Yep," Julian said.

Linda squinted her eyes at Julian and asked, "Ok, you mean what we do before we ask Him the first time to forgive us but not after we know better."

"Before, during and after we know," Julian answered.

"So we can just keep messing up no matter what?"

"Is that what you want to do?" Julian asked in an exasperated tone. "Do you want to keep messing up? Do you want to keep transgressing?

"No of course not." She answered. Julian gave her a look of, I rest my case. But Linda kept after him. "So you are saying that no matter what, no matter how many times we mess up, God will still forgive us?

"Do you just need confirmation of these things because you are repeating yourself?" Julian went over to the sofa and laid down. He started tossing the ball into the air again. He knew that Linda was getting around to what she really wanted to know.

"No, it's not that I need confirmation," Linda said. "It's just that if I have to accept it for myself then I have to accept it for other people as well."

"Yep," Julian responded. "If God is going to forgive you for whatever, he will do the same for all."

Linda looked into the air and folded her arms against her chest. She was hearing what Julian was saying but how could she forgive. She was still having nightmares. She could not get it out of her mind.

Years earlier

Carlos is sitting at the piano, with baby Dorian sitting in his lap. He was laughing as he was trying to show Dorian a chord but Dorian just banged on the keys. He hugs and kisses his son with much affection. He pulls his gaze to an upstairs room with closed doors.

"Hum, it's quiet up there now." He continues to play.

Upstairs in the room, an elderly man is standing there. He is using a handkerchief to clean blood off of his hands. After he finishes, he throws it at the feet of crumbled up legs that are coming from beside the bed. He looks down at them, smirks and leaves the room. The legs of the woman are not moving at first. The sound of a moan is heard and the legs begin to slowly move. Linda's hand and arm slowly come up and she lays it across the bed. She braces herself and lifts. Linda sits on the edge of the bed for a moment. She gets up and walks to the bathroom bent over holding her side. As she turns the faucet on, blood is dripping heavily into the sink. She takes a washcloth and begins to gingerly clean her face. The sink fills with blood as she wrings out the washcloth. She looks at herself in the mirror and begins to cry as she looked at the deep cuts, swollen eyes, lips and bruises that covered her face. Her sobbing stops when she hears Carlos, Dorian and the other man laughing and playing.

She hurriedly left the bathroom. She stands at the railing looking down into the living room. Her frail defeated look turned to one of disgust as she listened to her father-in-law.

Standing there with his knuckles covered in dried blood and taking a picture of Carlos and Dorian he says, "You shouldn't have any more trouble out of her. If you do, just handle it. Obedience is what you want from a woman." He picks up Dorian. "How is my big man huh? You're going to be like me and your Papi, eh?"

He tickles Dorian who is laughing but trying to get back to the piano. Carlos takes him back into his arms and Dorian begins to bang on the keys again. Determination exploded through the bruises on Linda's face and so does anger.

"I'll burn in hell first before I'll let either of you corrupt my son". She quietly steps back into the bedroom.

"That's what's hard for me," Linda said almost in a whisper as she continues her conversation with Julian.

He sat up and returned to his more gentle side. "Have you been hurt by someone?" He already knew the answer to that question but he knew that Linda's healing could not start until she admitted that she was hurt. But more importantly that she received validation. She does not answer his question and Julian could see that the peace that she had found earlier that evening was disappearing.

He walked over to her and said, "Linda, if God did not forgive all unconditionally, He could not be love. Besides, He wouldn't have anybody to talk to if he didn't forgive." Linda let out a little smile. Julian took her hands in his and looked into her eyes. "That's the kind of love He has. A love that knows no limits, a love that would die for you."

He put his arms around her and Linda melted into his chest. "Does that kind of love still exist?" She asked him.

"That kind of Love will always exist. And if your heart is open and full of forgiveness, that kind of Love will manifest for you."

Linda was still having a hard time with the forgiving 'everything' bit. "But forgive everything, Julian?" She cried. She wanted to do the right thing. The thing that God would want but she just did not think that she had the strength to.

Julian knew that she was struggling but he also knew that sugar coating or making light of it was not going to help her. "You know what helps me in this – I think about Jesus. No matter what people believe about Him, He is the greatest example of love and forgiveness that this world has ever known."

Linda listened to Julian intently. Somehow his words did not sound preachy. They were laced with sentiments that expressed true experience and emotion – not just something that he read in a book somewhere. His words began to penetrate the wounds in her heart that had been frozen in time.

Julian continued walking around the house full of passionate zeal as he talked about Jesus. "Here we have a man that was totally innocent of any evil. He was betrayed by someone close to him, taken and beaten beyond recognition. Tried and accuse unjustly. Humiliated as he had to drag a cross through a city of people he had just brought healing and blessing to. Those same people now were reviling Him. He was nailed to that cross - to that tree and you know what he does? He looks upon His murderers and prays to His Father in heaven, 'forgive them, Father, for they know not what they do'. If perfect innocence could extend that kind of forgiveness, how much more should we?"

Linda walked around – Julian's words were melting anyway the barriers that had been in her heart for so many years. "So like Jesus, we can extend forgiveness even in the midst of pain? Extend forgiveness even towards the one that caused the pain."

"Yes! Especially then, with the Holy Spirits help. And don't fear that it means you have to become a door mate. But that is another subject." Julian said.

Linda walked over to her makeshift desk. She pulled out some paper and began to write. Julian picked up a magazine from off of the table and the message that Mrs. Winder had put there the night before fell to the floor. He walked over to Linda so he did not see it. Julian noticed that Linda was in a good writing flow.

"You seem to be cooking now. Can I take a peek?"

 "Sure," Linda told him.

Julian read what she had written so far. He was amazed. "Your words are elegant Linda."

"I hope Mr. Giles thinks so."

Julian put his hand on her shoulder. "Let me share something with you. If your words come from your heart as directed by God – it will affect those for whom it is meant." He squeezed her shoulder giving it a little shake. "That's all that matters."

Linda mused for a moment. "What if I get writers' block?"

Julian acted as if he had fainted and fell to the floor. With his hands over his eyes, he said, "Lord keep me near the cross. I believe that God can bring inspiration." He got up off of the floor. "Now enough talk. Continue writing. I think that I am going to go for a walk."

Linda whirls her head looking up from her desk. "You're leaving?" She wailed.

Julian headed towards the door. "I'll be back. Just going to get some of God's good night air. Handle your business."

28

Julian left the house and stepped out on the porch. He waved at Mrs. Winder, who was sitting on her porch as she normally did this time of night. She waved back. Julian walked down the steps and began his trek up the street. Down the street opposite from the way Julian was walking, the dark Mercedes turned into the neighborhood. The Driver and Carlos got out of the car. They parked a little way down the street and ran behind the houses in the neighborhood towards Linda's. Julian thinking he had heard something behind him turned to look. He did not see anything so he continued with his walk. He turned the corner out of view of Linda's house.

Linda was still writing when Dorian came running into the living room from his room. "I got it! I got it, mom!" Dorian yelled animatedly to his mother.

Linda stopped writing. "You got what baby?"

"This song that I have been trying to learn. Can I play it for you? Please?"

"Sure you can baby." Linda did not ever remember seeing her son so excited about a song before.

Dorian looked around the room. "Where is Julian? I want him to hear it too."

"He went out for a walk." She got up and went to look out of the window for him but she did not see him. She looked across the street and noticed that Mrs. Winder was not sitting on the porch.

"Hum, that's strange."

"What is mommy?" Dorian asked.

"Nothing baby. I don't see Julian right now. He'll be back but you can play it for me in the meantime."

"Ok." Dorian ran to go get his keyboard. Linda noticed the paper on the floor and picked it up. She was about to read it when Dorian came back into the room and set up his keyboard. "Are you ready for this?" Dorian inquired of his mother.

"I sure am," Linda responded smiling at the enthusiasm of her son. She still had the paper in her hand and had not read it yet. Dorian started playing the song and a look of horror shadowed over Linda's face. It had been years but she had not forgotten that song. She remembered the man who played it every time before he beat her.

"Dorian?" Linda screamed out his name causing him to stop playing abruptly.

"What's wrong mom?"

"Where did you learn that song?" She was yelling so loud and incoherently that Dorian could not understand her. Linda's actions were also scaring Dorian. He had never seen his mother this enraged before.

"What?" Dorian asked trying to understand her.

Linda grabbed Dorian, shaking and yelling at him. "Where did you learn that song?"

Dorian started to cry. "Mom you're hurting me."

"Where did you learn it?"

"At school. This man taught me."

"What man?"

"I don't know. He came to my class. He just started talking to me and played this song. He taught me some of it and then left. That's all. I mean it!"

Linda's eyes were bloodshot red. "Did he come here? Dorian, did he come here?" Dorian told her no and restated that his mom was hurting him. Linda let him go and slowly look at the paper in her hand. Linda tried to read the paper but the words were blurry because of her agitation. She rubbed her eyes and shook her head to clear it. The words of the message became clear as Mrs. Winders' handwriting came into focus. Linda, someone called here for Luminosa Andres.

Linda dropped the paper to the floor. "Dorian, come on we have to get out of here baby."

"Why mom?" Dorian was scared, not knowing what to do.

"Don't ask me any questions right now we just have to get out of here now!" Linda grabbed Dorian's hand and they ran toward the back rooms of the house. Out of nowhere, Carlos jumped out of the shadows. The sudden appearance of him caused Linda to let Dorian go. Carlos seized her and put a knife to her throat.

"Hello, Luminosa darling. It's been a long time." There was a familiar evil in his eyes that Linda recognized. An evil that she had run away from.

Dorian began to kick Carlos to free his mother from Carlos's grip. "Let my mother go. Take your hands off of her." The Driver came up and snatched Dorian from behind.

Linda yelled, "No Please don't hurt him!"

"Leave my mom alone you butt head," Dorian yelled at Carlos as he continued to struggle with the man who was holding him. The man squeezed a little tighter and Dorian yelled out in pain.

"Please!" Linda again pleaded.

Carlos pressed the point of the knife harder into Linda's neck and it drew blood. "Shut –up." He told her. He looked in Dorian's direction. "Now Dorian, is that any way for you to talk to your father?"

"You're not my father. My father is dead." Dorian yelled.

"Luminosa, have you lied to our son, our love child?" He kissed her on the cheek and dragged her back into the living room. She fell to the ground and tried to crawl towards Dorian and the Driver. Carlos caught her by the ankle and pulled her back towards him. She hit her head against the leg of her desk and blood ran down her face. Carlos picked her up and slapped her and threw her on the couch.

"Don't hit my mom!" Dorian yelled. He then bit the Driver's hand drawing blood.

The man screamed in pain. "You little brat!" He yelled in Spanish.

He was getting ready to hit him but looked up at Carlos and thought better of it. Carlos gave a look of warning to the Driver and said, "My son amigo, don't you forget that." The Driver let Dorian go and he ran to his mother who was sitting on the couch bleeding.

"Get out of here. Leave us alone!" Dorian yelled.

Carlos smiled. "He's got a lot of fire - a lot of nerve. I guess I have to admit that he got that from you." The smile disappeared from Carlos's face. He got very close to Linda's face. "You know why? Because you must have a lot of nerve to have left me and stolen my son. My son!"

He put the knife in her face. Linda tried to retreat from the menacing blade. "Did you really think that you could run forever? Did you? No one runs out on Carlos Andres. Do you understand that?" Carlos stood up and paced the floor.

He continued talking. "You know, I was just going to come here, get my son and leave. No drama. But guess what? My son did not even know that I was alive." He kicked over the coffee table. Magazines and the coffee cups that Linda and Julian were drinking out of earlier went flying across the room. He also knocked over the book self. The Bible fell to the floor and Dorian's birth certificate with the parent's names listed as Carlos and Luminosa Andres fell out.

Carlos saw it and picked it up. As he read it, he began to shake squeezing it in his hands. "That makes me crazy. It makes me want to hurt something. To cause the same pain that not having my son for the last 10 years has caused me." He threw the paper down and stepped behind the sofa and put the knife to Linda's throat again and whispered in her ear.

"Do you know that kind of pain Luminosa? How could you? Your son was not stolen from you. No. You did the stealing." Carlos yanked her head back by her hair. "Do you know pain like that?"

Linda stopped cowering even with the knife at her throat. She would not bow down to his threats any longer. She answered him with strength in her voice. "Yes. Yes, I do know pain. It's the pain of love withheld by your husband. It's the pain of being struck by him over and over again. It's the pain of knowing the love that by covenant is only suppose to belong to you, is being given to another. It's the pain of instead of a husband's protection, he lets another beat her. I know the torment of wondering if those same sick actions will befall my son as well. Yes, I know pain."

Carlos pressed the knife harder still to her neck. "Are you mocking me?"

"No, I'm just answering your question, Carlos." He laughed at her and tried to stroke Dorian's hair but Dorian pulled away.

"I thought we were amigos?" Carlos said to Dorian.

"If you were my friend, you wouldn't hurt my mom."

"Once again there are things that you are not old enough to understand. You'll come with me and I'll teach you."

"I am not going anywhere with you. You're twisted." Dorian said as he glared at him.

"Kids got a nasty mouth. I guess you think he got that from me."

Linda began to plead with Carlos. Not because she was afraid. She was concerned about the well being of her son. "Carlos, please. Let us go."

Carlos jumped up in a rage. "You don't get it, do you. I'm not here for you. I could care less about an ungrateful witch who stole my son." He walked back over to her and stroked his knife down the front of her top. "Tonight you, as a thorn in my flesh, will be removed and I will leave with my son." He stood up and said to the Driver, "Take him out of the room."

The man walked over to Dorian and tried to pick him up. Dorian yelled and kicked and screamed. Linda clawed at the man's arms. The man dropped Dorian in pain and backhanded Linda. Dorian got up and ran into Carlos making him trip over the table that he had turned over earlier. Dorian ran towards the door and ran out of the house.

"Run baby run! Go get help for momma."

Carlos was on his hands and knees as he yelled to the Driver "Go get him!"

The man bolted for the door to go after Dorian. Just as the man was about to run out Julian came through the door and tackled him. A big fight ensued. Both men were beating Julian. Linda tried to help but Carlos hit her hard. She slammed into the wall and crumbled to the floor. Carlos and the Driver continued to beat Julian almost to the point of unconsciousness. Julian was lying on the floor in a puddle of blood when Carlos picked him up. The Driver drew a knife of his own. He was getting ready to stab Julian when the sound of a gunshot rang out. Driver's eyes widened and he dropped his knife and fell to the floor. Behind him, Mrs. Winder stood with a smoking gun.

Carlos screamed at her. "Old woman…" He started to throw his knife at her, but Linda hit him from behind with the crucifix. He fell to the ground as blood gushed out of his head. Linda hit him again. He squirmed in pain.

"How does it feel to be hit, huh?" She hit him again. "You threaten me and my son." Linda was in a rage. Every time she hit Carlos she remembered every blow that he had given her. She was blinded by fury and struck him again and again and again. Julian's hands began to move as he pushed himself up off of the ground. He crawled to the papers that have been thrown to the floor. He found the paper that Linda had been working on earlier that night. He crawled over to Linda who was still hitting Carlos. Carlos's blood was splashing onto her face.

Julian reached up to stop her. He was barely able to speak but he said, "Linda if you kill him, you will never be able to finish this." Julian began to cough up blood. She looked at Julian, as he held on tighter to her. "Love gave its life for you tonight. Now return the favor." Linda started to cry. She could not let Carlos continue to have control over her by taking his life. The only way to rid herself of his control over her was to let him live. She dropped the crucifix and put Julian's head in her lap. The sound of sirens could be heard in the air. Dorian had called the police from Mrs. Winder's house. Mrs. Winder had gone outside to make sure they knew where to come.

He looked up at Linda and said, "Mercy is always better than revenge." He closed his eyes. His breathing became shallow.

The police came running into the house along with the paramedics. A police officer escorted Linda out while the paramedics began to work on Julian and a battered Carlos.

"My son…"

"He is just fine.'' The police officer said to reassure her. When they got outside she saw Mrs. Winder. She walked over to her. She was answering some questions for the police. They hugged and spoke to each other without saying any words. At that moment Linda heard Dorian's voice.

"Mom."

Linda turned and ran over to her son and embraced him. "I am so sorry baby. I am so sorry."

Dorian looked at her and took off his shirt and began to wipe the blood off of her face. "Why, for loving me. Protecting me. I don't understand everything but I do understand this - True love is unconditional even when you are wronged."

Linda looked at her son once again amazed. "Is that what I taught you?"

"No mom. That's what you showed me." Linda and Dorian continued to hug as Julian was brought out on a stretcher and the Driver in a body bag. Carlos was brought out in handcuffs. He looked over at Linda and Dorian. They both stared back at him as a united front. Carlos dropped his head as a policeman put him into a squad car. A paramedic came over to tend to Linda's wounds. He was a very handsome man. Linda saw a strangely familiar look in his eyes.

"Here let me take a look at that cut." He touched her gently but Linda could feel the strength in his hands. She attempted to act like she did not need any help.

"I'm ok. I just need a band-aid."

The Paramedic chastised her. "Will you stop trying to control everything thing in your life and let me help you." Linda stared at the man in disbelief. Those were the exact words that Julian had spoken to her earlier that day except for the let me help you. She sat back and decided to receive his help and let him finish. Again she tried to place those familiar eyes of his.

He looked at Dorian and said, "Hey bud do you want to be my helper?"

"Sure!" Dorian said with genuine excitement in his voice. The two of them cleaned up her wounds. They finished and the Paramedic went back to his truck to return his equipment. She and Dorian were talking but looked up when they heard the sound of the siren of the ambulance that Julian was in. They watched as the ambulance dashed out of the neighborhood. A policeman came over to get some more information for his report. The emergency crew was leaving the scene but her neighbors were beginning to gravitate towards her. The police officer finished and asked Linda if she felt the need for a patrol car to stay in the area. She looked around at all of her neighbors. She knew they would look out for her and her son so she told him no that it would not be necessary - they were fine.

He left. Homer and his wife, Mrs. Winder and many others gathered around her and Dorian. You could feel a real sense of community. Linda knew that she was not alone. But what surprised her most was that as she and Dorian were returning to their home, the handsome Paramedic was sitting on her steps. Linda approached him.

The young man rose, as she got closer. "Ma'am, I figured that you might need some help cleaning up - you and your boy. Since I have nothing else to do or no one else to get home to - I thought that maybe I could help." Linda did not say anything. He put his hands in his pocket - let out a nervous smile and said, "I'm sorry. I don't know what I was thinking. I'll let. I'll just leave. Good night ma'am." He stepped off of the porch smiled at Dorian and began to walk away. He felt really stupid because he let his partner leave and his partner was driving. As he was walking down the street, telling himself how stupid he was, he heard her voice.

"Hey, what do you take in your coffee?"

He turned and smiled at her and answered, "Tons of cream and sugar." He walked back.

"How did I know that was what you were going to say? One thing though. Please call me Linda. My name is not ma'am."

"Ok, only if you call me yours." Linda blushed. "But if you need some time you can just call me Jael." Linda smiled and headed through the door and held it open for Jael. He picked Dorian up and put him on his shoulders and they went back into the house.

29

It was early Sunday morning. Linda was standing looking around at all of the activity going on. The bandage on her head and a few other bruises served as reminders of what she had triumphed over the night before. For her, those bruises were a badge of honor and sign of overcoming instead of signs of shame.

Salomé walked up behind Linda but called out to her in an effort not to scare her. "Linda."

Linda turned and saw Salomé. "Hi." She responded.

They embraced one another and stayed silent for a few moments. "My God," Salomé said, breaking the silence. "I heard what happened. Are you Ok?"

"I am great as a matter of fact," Linda said to her with a sincere smile on her face.

"How about your son, how is he?"

"That little trooper is fine. He's my little hero."

"I was surprised when you called this morning and left the message to say that you would be here and already had your project determined and started."

"Julian would want it that way," Linda said. "I believe that he would say that we cannot let the demons of our past stop our God-given gifts from being shared with the world."

"Or our critics stop us," Salomé added. They walked hand in hand towards the garden area of the hotel.

Cameron was finishing up reading the letter that Julian had left for him as he and Mr. Giles arrived at the hospital to check on him.

Cameron,

Continue to be the man that you are. The type of man that women need. Let your hands always be to her a source of love and strength. Be the one for her that will protect her from those evil dragons that seek to devour. Be her watchman ever watching out for her from the Lord's tower. A situation may arise and she will need your help.

Cameron folded the letter up and put it in his pocket. They continued to walk to Julian's room. When they arrived however he was not there.

"Cameron, are you sure that this is the room?"

"Yes, sir." He replied checking the room number. "This is the room they said.

They walked over to the nurse's station. "Excuse me, nurse," Cameron said getting the attention of the charge nurse. "Where is the patient that is supposed to be in that room?"

The nurse looked in the room that Cameron was pointing to and said, "There's no patient in that room."

"Well, we can see that. We want to know where he is." Cameron replied.

"I'm sorry but there hasn't been anyone assigned to that room for the past 3 days."

"Ok then. Can you just tell us what room Mr. Julian Noel is in please?" Asked Mr. Giles.

The nurse typed Julian's name into the computer. "I'm sorry but we have no one here by that name."

"You mean he has checked out already?" Cameron asked.

"No. I mean no one by that name has been checked in here or out." The nurse answered. Cameron and Mr. Giles look at each other dazed.

30

The hotel garden area was full of symposium attendees for the closing ceremonies. Linda was on the stage giving a speech. The crowd listened attentively to the woman who just the night before was facing death and had defeated it triumphantly.

"If someone had told me a couple of days ago that on the third day of this symposium, I would be standing here, I would have told them that they were crazy." She looked out at her audience to see Salomé, her son, Mrs. Winder, and Jael smiling up at her.

"Well actually, just a couple of days ago no one would have said anything to me because I was so shut off from everything and everybody. But thanks to a brilliant woman, my son, a baby sitter, a new friend and a heavenly stranger all that has changed." She lowered her head trying to keep the tears from flowing. She so wanted Julian to be there.

"That stranger showed me that my fears and bitterness were killing me. He gave me the strength to move beyond all the guilt and even amid pain, to reach for and receive the love of God. A love that looks beyond our faults." She paused as she thought for a moment of Carlos. "All of our faults. So I dedicate this first installment of my soon to be released book of poetry, 'Blossom of a Mended Rose', to my son and the heart of my consciousness, Julian Noel."

She took a piece of bloody paper from her purse. She unfolded it and began to read it to the audience.

I Extend

With your looks and whispers, you kick to bring me down. You swing and land a punch to crush me - Silence turns to thunder by its sound. You tear at me to rid yourself of what you consider as 'my disease.' 'You have no place here' you surmise as you continue to beat me. With every curse and words filled with hate, you try to smash the reflection of yourself that you see. You snarl 'you are a misfit, you are marred' and you hit me again - Your actions animating this decree.

Well, beat on If you like and in the breeze, you will hear my laughter. I know the truth, my hopes you can never shatter. Jesus above has given me a place through the blood he shed and the water that poured from his side. For misfits like me, he hung on the cross, for one such as me he died. God gives for all who would believe - so-called normal and misfit alike. To Them He gives His grace - He gives

Eternal Life. You on the other hand freely give me your fist, but if you knew Him, you would offer me your prayers instead. Not wishing that you could rid yourself of me. Not wishing that I was dead.

You try to knock me down, but I see Him standing there so I rise. He does not see what you see. Only His love for me - for us all fills His eyes. That same love fills my heart for you no matter what you do. You see, He loved me first in spite of myself and I Extend the same to you."

She finished and returned the paper to her purse. The silence was interrupted only by the sniffles of those who could not hold back their tears.

Linda continued to speak. "For me, in my life and heart, fear no longer has a home. Only love abides there. Someone was an instrument of that love for me. I pray that I may become an instrument as well. Because love is the only thing that will make a difference."

Across from the garden on the beach sat a familiar figure on some rocks. Julian was writing in his notebook with no sign of injury or trauma at all to his body. On the page written in the prettiest color of blue, 'No more havoc in Havocy Bay." Julian closed the notebook tied a cord around it and put it in the satchel.

"Well, it is finished. All is restored. Where to next Lord?" He bowed his head in prayer. After a moment he climbed down off of the rocks and began to walk away. Linda was now talking among the crowd and signing autographs along with a jubilant Dorian and Jael by her side. A dove drifted over to where they were. A gentle breeze blew over them as the dove hovered for a moment. Dorian looked up and saw the dove. They made eye contact. Dorian closed his eyes and listened to the fluttering of its wings. He opened his eyes and watched as the bird flew away.

He continued to watch the dove as it disappeared over the horizon of the ocean. A single tear ran down his cheek as he waved to the dove and quietly said, "Good-bye Julian – I will never forget you."